POINT LAST SEEN

STEVEN GALE

DEDICATION

To Hannah and Aaron, you two are my heroes.
To my wife, Sally, and our five grandkids.
DREAM BIG AND DARE TO FAIL.

First paperback edition October 2024
First ebook edition October 2024
Print ISBN 978-1-7367487-5-6
Ebook 978-1-7367487-6-3

Book cover and interior design by JohnEdgar.Design
Published by Agragape Publications

POINT LAST SEEN

MANGLER3

STEVEN GALE
STORYTELLER & AUTHOR

As a kid Steven would hide behind his dad's chair during the TV show 'The Night Stalker'. Having grown up during arguably the best era in motion picture history, he believes that helped him develop the art of storytelling. He feels today's special effects have robbed people of developing their own imagination.

Steven is the father of a combat veteran and a Military Police veteran and husband to a wonderful wife. He loves hiking in the mountains and doing research for upcoming Mangler books.

POINT
LAST
SEEN

STEVEN GALE

CONTENTS

Mangler = to lack, to be short of, to be without,
to be lacking, to be missing

Danish dictionary

Recap
BOOK I

Doyle and Scotty have been steadily moving west. They both are decked out in their rain-proof gear with hooded ponchos. The first few hours, it was downhill into the water runoff from the Noland Divide; then, it's been back uphill towards Jim Ute Ridge for the past few hours.

Doyle sits on a large fallen tree trunk and takes his water bottle from the pack. "Scotty! Come over here and rest a minute."

"Okay. I'm on my way," replies Scotty as he walks over and sits on the same log, "Man, my feet are killing me."

"I'll trade you my fifty-year-old feet," Doyle tells him.

After taking several drinks, Scotty leans down to loosen his left bootstrap. "What have we here? Look, Doyle, a footprint," he said,

pointing at the footprint near his boot, a mysterious clue in the vast forest.

Doyle kneels to inspect the footprint. "Yeah, that's his track. It looks like he stepped off this log and right back on it. It's like he's traveling up in the trees. Otherwise, With all this rain, there should be tracks everywhere." Doyle starts looking closely at the trees around the log. "If an animal is carrying him, there should be signs."

Scotty frowns, thinking about Doyle's words, "Have you ever seen that?"

"Only once, and there was blood everywhere. It was in the Adirondack mountains in 2014 when I was a Forest Ranger with the State of New York," replied Doyle, turning to Scotty. "Scotty, place two small red flags near the tracks while I search the area."

Near the base of a large tree, he finds an impression about four inches deep, as if something heavy had been set down there. Doyle squats down and places his hand softly on the mark, saying, "Look at this, Scotty."

"It looks a lot like the shape of a Christmas ornament," Scotty says.

Doyle stood up and gazed up to the tree top, "What could the boy have in his pack that would make a print like this? Even if he stood on it, it wouldn't sink this deep. I wonder if there was a mark like this back at the…"

The forest falls into an eerie stillness, the silence broken only by the sound of the light rain. The hairs all over Doyle's body stand up. He

hears Scotty gasp and say, "Doyle…" He slowly reaches into his poncho and pulls out his 9mm. He positions himself on one knee and scans the area, looking for anything that seems out of place.

As the rain starts collecting on his glasses, Doyle wrinkles up his nose just enough to make the glasses slide down so he can look over them. Out of the corner of his left eye, he notices a slight movement and slowly turns his head in that direction. Approximately fifteen feet off the ground and very close to a tree trunk, Doyle sees what looks to be an area of blurred light. The rain falling between him and the blur amplifies the light in that area, adding to the mystery. He can see further down the valley except when looking at this spot. He tries to focus on this area, but it remains a blur.

"Scotty, are you reflecting a mirror up there?"

"No, I'm…I'm not doing anything."

Doyle's eyes flicker to Scotty, who is frozen in place, before returning to the strange figure. It's not just light; it's a shimmering, almost translucent figure. It moves without a sound, shifting to the other side of the tree as if it's a living being.

Slowly, Doyle turns his shoulders to aim his 9mm at the spot, wondering if the rain and the afternoon light are just playing tricks on him. "What the hell is that?"

Neither he nor the spot of light moves as if each one knows the other is looking directly at them. He considers firing a shot near it to

see if it would move again when a woman yelling echoes through the forest from behind them.

Doyle's head whips around towards the source of the yelling. They must be closer to Noland Creek Trail than he initially thought. When he turns back to the tree, the strange light is gone. His hands shake with adrenaline, like after a near-miss car accident. "Scotty. Scotty!"

Scotty is still standing there, frozen. He slowly looks over at Doyle. "What was that?"

"I'm not sure. Did you see where it went?" asked Doyle.

"Yeah, it slid down the tree and ran off in that direction," Scotty replies, pointing to the south.

The forest is coming back to life. The rain has stopped, and birds are moving around and calling. They hear the woman again and realize she's out looking for Allen with the volunteers.

"Hey, guys, wait up! I think I found some footprints," she shouted.

Doyle starts to jog, "Come on, Scotty!" When they reach the trail, they see four young people kneeling just off the side of it.

"What did you find?" Doyle asks.

One of the young men turns to face Doyle. "Sir, it looks like shoe tracks." The other volunteers nod in agreement, their eyes wide with anticipation.

Doyle kneels to get a closer look. The tracks do match the ones he's been following. "Look here, Scotty. See this spot in the track? Allen

has a small chunk of the sole missing from his left shoe." Doyle turns towards the young people, "Yep, those are the missing boy's tracks. Good job guys." The discovery of the footprints brings a glimmer of hope to the search.

The two ladies with the group give each other a high-five. Doyle drops his pack on the trail and reaches into a pocket to retrieve a red flag. He stands up and smiles at the group, "Y'all should continue down the trail. Maybe you'll catch up with him."

"Yes, Sir, we will! Come on. Let's go!" says one of the young ladies as they head south down the trail.

Doyle watches them go around a curve. One of the young men, who has two speakers hanging on his backpack, turns on some music, and the song echoes through the region.

Doyle smiles when he hears it, then staggers as he reaches out and supports his weight against a tree.

Scotty reaches over and grabs his arm, "Easy, Doyle. Are you dizzy?"

"Yeah, just a bit." Doyle sits down with his back to the tree.

Scotty sits down on the opposite side of the trail, "Should I call someone for help?"

"No, I'll be okay. When I heard that song, I had a solid memory pop up in my head. I could even smell the candles from a store nearby that night."

"What was the memory?" Scotty asks.

"That song was Tom Petty's, Even the losers," Doyle tells him as he looks at the red flag, still in his hand.

Scotty nods, "Great song."

"It was December of 1979. My parents had taken my sisters, Katie and Hannah, and me to the mall in Knoxville, Tennessee. Katie and I walked down to the record shop, but Hannah was still too young to go with us," Doyle explained. "I had only one thing on my mind: find the new Tom Petty Album. When I picked that album up… Damn the Torpedoes. Petty was on the front holding a Rickenbacker twelve-string. I remember it like it was yesterday."

"That's cool. I wish we had records when I was growing up," says Scotty.

"Those were the days. It's not like today when you can just download a song. We had to wait for the album to come out. Sometimes, they'd release a 45 with an A-side hit single and a B-side song."

"Are these flashbacks part of your PTSD?"

"That's what they say. An anxiety disorder." Doyle tells him as he stands back up.

He realizes it's time to return to work, so he walks over and places the red flag beside the footprint. "Allen just crossed over the trail. He didn't turn south and follow it downhill."

"Why wouldn't he follow the trail? I don't get it," Scotty says.

"Many researchers believe that, when someone is lost, they get so disoriented that they won't even recognize a trail. Another factor that we're probably dealing with is a medical event. Since he crossed this trail, we'll mark this as the last known point (LKP). Let's sweep this area for any more signs. Then we need to find a place to camp. It'll be dark soon," Doyle explains. "We have maybe an hour of daylight left."

Both of their radios squawked. "Come in, Doyle. This is Joe."

"This is Doyle. Go ahead."

"Doyle, the park rangers are off-trail searching towards the Noland Creek trail. Once they reach that trail, they will stop at the Backcountry Camp number 65. Are you two camping there as well?"

"No, Joe. We're going deeper in the bush, probably once we reach the Laurel Branch ridge."

"Doyle, have you found anything?"

"Yes. We found tracks one hundred yards east of Noland Creek trail, which we marked. Then more crossing over the trail, which we marked as the LKP."

"Great find, Doyle. The K9s will start there in the morning. I'd send them now, but the weather is about to get worse. The heavy rain should be out of the area by morning. All the connecting trails have been searched multiple times. The Green Berets have set up camp at Deep Creek, near Bryson City."

"Okay, Joe. Thanks for the update; I'll check in with you in the morning," replied Doyle.

"Sounds good, Doyle. Joe out."

"Ten-four. Doyle out."

"Scotty, I think we're done here. Let's get moving. I want to reach the ridge before the rain sets in. I know of a perfect bluff area to set up our tents."

"I'm right behind you, Doyle," Scotty said, quickly walking to catch up with Doyle.

```
0300 HOURS
07 SEPTEMBER * ALLEN WOLFGANG'S SAR -  LAST YEAR
GREAT SMOKY MOUNTAINS - CAMPSITE
```

Doyle's watch is vibrating. It's his alarm, set to 0300. He jumps out of the dream he was having, confused, and looks around, trying to figure out where he is.

He climbs out of his sleeping bag and tent, grabs his boots, and pulls them on.

"I'm getting too old for this stuff," he says out loud.

At that moment, he hears someone walking down in the valley. He grabs his night vision goggles and climbs on the rocks near his tent. Looking through them, he sees four men in camouflage clothing moving through the valley below him.

"What are these guys doing? Are they Green Berets?" He watches them for a while and notices they are searching in the trees. They also have night vision and use it to look up the trees.

"What are they looking for in the trees?"

Doyle watches them until they go out of sight to his right, which is west. That's the direction he and Scotty are working, but while staying on the high ground, these guys are down in the valley.

He climbs back down and opens Scotty's tent. "Hey. It's time to get up, but be very quiet."

"What's going on?" Scotty asks.

"I'm going to go check something out. I want you to pack your gear up and ensure no hot embers are left in the fire pit. I'll come back to get you in about fifteen minutes." Doyle explains as he rolls up his tent and sleeping bag and puts them in his backpack.

Doyle grabs his walking stick but leaves his night vision on his hat. After grabbing a handful of beef jerky and a bottle of water, he starts after those men. After about a hundred yards, Doyle turns west to better view the men, who know how to move through the forest quietly, but for some reason, these guys aren't bothered to do the same.

Still on the ridge, Doyle pauses to scan the area with his night vision. "What in the hell were they looking for in the trees? Do they know something we don't? And why was the FBI called in? Has Joe talked to the FBI?" Doyle is questioning everything that doesn't add

up. His frustration is palpable, but his unwavering determination to uncover the truth keeps him going. He sighs, "I will find out."

He heads downhill to catch up with the guys, knowing he can move up on them without them even knowing he is around. It only takes him fifteen minutes to slip through the forest before he hears them moving around. Doyle stays on the higher ground to have the best view. Doyle notices they stopped near a large sugar maple tree, and one of the guys was climbing up in it.

Looking through the night vision, he notices that all four men are wearing Army-issued ACUs (Army Combat Uniforms), which means they are Green Berets.

"Yeah, there's a few of those same marks up here," one Berets says from up in the tree.

"Okay. Take a few pictures of it and come back down," called one of the Berets on the ground.

Doyle sees the flicker of the camera flash, and then the Beret climbs down. The group heads off again, and as Doyle starts to stand up to follow them, he suddenly feels the cold touch of a pistol barrel against the back of his head.

The thought runs through Doyle's mind to take this guy out, but this is not war. He stands up and turns around. "Miller. I thought I smelled dog crap earlier," Doyle said as he saw Colonel Miller holding the firearm pointed at him.

"Funny Anderson. Always the funny guy. But you're getting sloppy with old age; I could have killed you, and you'd never seen it coming."

"You don't have it in you. By the way, the last time you pointed a gun at me, I broke two of your ribs," Doyle replies, smiling at him.

"Oh, I remember. I still owe you for that."

Unknown to Doyle, Scotty didn't stay at the campsite. He is lying atop a ridge, watching with cheap night vision goggles.

Doyle takes a step towards him. "You don't owe me anything; I still owe you for Bullseye's death. Don't think for a second that I've forgotten." His defiance towards Colonel Miller is palpable, adding intensity to their conflict.

"Yeah, I know. Still carrying that burden with you, I see. I never could understand that. You guys are expendable. Don't you know that?"

Doyle smiles, shaking his head. "I never could understand how someone who wore the uniform could become a politician's yes man. Now, I'll give you two seconds to point that gun somewhere else, or it's going to get ugly. One... two..."

"Okay, Anderson. Probably wasn't the best way to say hi to some-one with PTSD – some nutcase like you." Colonel Miller lowers the gun and puts it back in its holster. "Why were you watching my men?"

Doyle takes another step towards Miller. "Just seeing what they were up to. That's all."

"Don't give me that. You're supposed to be searching for that lost kid. Not spying on my men."

Doyle just stands there looking at him. Colonel Miller finally asks, "Have you found anything interesting out here tonight?"

Doyle shakes his head. "Just a pile of dog crap, like I said."

"There you go again, Anderson. You're a cantankerous old bastard, aren't you?"

"What are your men looking for?" asks Doyle.

Colonel Miller smiled, "We're training, that's all."

"Training for what?" Doyle presses, sensing more to the story than Miller is letting on.

"Oh, you know. Seeing how well you civilians can find a lost boy. And that reminds me: I meant to ask you why you couldn't stay away; you left active duty in 2000 and then turned around and did ten missions as a civilian contractor up to 2011. Was it for the money? Or because you enjoy killing? I think it was the killing. Am I right?"

"Why do you care?" Doyle asks, stepping closer again.

"Easy, big boy," Miller says, stepping back. "You would have been great, Anderson, if only you didn't have to always follow the rules. And then there's caring for your men the way you did. Does South Africa keep you up at night?"

"I never talk about that. It goes with me to the grave. I followed orders. Period!"

"Yeah, but -" Colonel Miller started before Doyle cut him off.

"There are no buts, Miller! While we're at it, why don't you tell me what you have done to this young boy missing?"

"What? We have no part in that. You guys are searching for him, and we are studying you and your search and rescue crew."

"Bullshit, Miller. What's really going on here? Another one of your black-ops missions?"

"Oh, Anderson, you really need to get some help. You're making stuff up in your mind now. How's the PTSD? You hearing or seeing people yet?"

Doyle laughs out loud. "Tell me. Why is the FBI here?"

"I have no clue. I told you, we're here to conduct training in what not to do. Listen - you've wasted enough of my time. You go right ahead and continue your little search for that boy. And if I catch you near my team again, I'll have you arrested. Understand, Anderson?" With that, Miller backed away and headed off into the darkness.

"Understand this, Colonel. If you ever point a gun at me again, you better have your soul ready. You hear me?"

Colonel Miller just laughed. "Oh, how I pray that day comes, Anderson. In the meantime, get some help, man. You're sick."

Doyle stood listening to Miller walk off into the forest. "Damn. That guy is like an STD or something. I never thought I'd bump into him out here. That changes everything now. They only use him for cover-up jobs. So, what in the hell is going on here?"

He looks at his watch, 0428. The sun will rise soon, and Doyle feels he has accomplished nothing this morning. He walks back towards the campsite to get the remainder of his gear. "

Why were they looking in the trees? And why was Miller lying in wait for me?" Clenching his fists, "I should have shot that bastard right on the spot - pointing a damn gun at me."

"Doyle! What the hell was that about?" Scotty asks, walking down the ridge.

"Why are you here? I told you to stay at the camp."

"I wanted to see what was going on. That Colonel guy was holding you at gunpoint. Why?"

"Don't worry about him. Come on, let's get our gear and get back on the search," says Doyle.

"Who was that guy?" asked Scotty.

"He was one of the commanders from Afghanistan. I did six deployments with him through the years. He's a prick!" Doyle said, laughing.

"I thought he was going to shoot you. I almost pulled my gun and shot at him," Scotty tells him.

Doyle stops. "I'm glad you didn't. His men would have killed you."

The two guys grab all their gear from the campsite and turn west to continue looking for the lost boy. "I'd like to reach the White Oak Branch trail by sunrise. I think there is something strange going on." Doyle explains.

"Like what?" Scotty asks.

"That guy is only used for black-ops missions. With him here, I think there's a mission going on."

"What's a black-ops mission?" asks Scotty.

"One you'll never find records of. Most of the time, the missions break the law. Normally killing some dictator or political enemy." Doyle tells him.

Scotty looked shocked. "They run these types of operations in the United States?"

Doyle stops walking and turns to look at him. Of course they do! I could tell you things you wouldn't believe."

"Like what?" asks Scotty.

"A few years ago, that young man who downloaded things off the Democratic National Committee's server and gave it to that website overseas. Remember how they said he was killed in a robbing? Yet, his wallet and phone were still on him, and he was shot in the back."

"Wow. That was a black op hit?" Scotty asks.

"It was. First, you must understand that the media is part of the problem. They never report facts, only propaganda." Doyle says, reaching down to turn off his two-way radio.

"Never trust anyone who works for the government. Even if you think they are a good guy. You never know who may be blackmailing them to get to you," explained Doyle.

```
2 130 HOURS
THIS PAST WINTER * AFTER SAR FOR JONAH
EDWARDS AIR FORCE BASE. CALIFORNIA
```

"Welcome to Edwards, Doyle," Jonah tells him as he helps him off the Blackhawk.

"Thanks, buddy," Doyle says, grabbing his hand.

"Doyle, Are you good to walk?"

"Yes, this brace feels so much better," he tells Jonah as they follow Mike into a nearby hangar. Doyle turns and watches the Blackhawk lift off the ground and fly out of sight to the west.

"Doyle, come on in. The doors are getting ready to close," Mike tells him as a warning alarm starts beeping. Doyle steps in but still looks outside: "What are those lights to the south that look hanging in the air?"

Jonah walks up to him. "That's Mountain High ski resort; many people think it's a UFO the first time they visit Edwards."

"Yeah, I remember that now," Doyle replies.

"Come on, let's get going. There are a lot of things I want to show you. This hangar wasn't here back in February 1954," Jonah explains.

"What happened in 1954?" Doyle asks.

Jonah stops at the top of a set of stairs leading down. "President Eisenhower came here to meet with a small group of extraterrestrials. This place was called Muroc Airfield back then. He came to this very set of stairs," Jonah says to him, pointing at the steps and emphasizing the location's historical significance.

The three men start down the stairway, with Mike leading the way. "Back then, the steps just led to a series of bunkers, but in the sixty-plus years since, we have built an entire underground base and city," Jonah tells Doyle, highlighting the secrecy of the underground base.

After two flights, they stop by a door, and Jonah unlocks it, "This is the very room where Eisenhower met with the aliens. This is also the actual door that one of the aliens stood guard at," explains Jonah, accentuating the room's unique features.

"Are you screwing with me?" Doyle asks him.

"Absolutely not!" snapped Jonah.

Doyle walks over and looks at the pictures hanging on the wall. He sees President Eisenhower standing in between two blonde-haired pale men. Their lips have no color, and there is no sign of facial hair. "What did they want?" Doyle asks.

"They wanted to sign a treaty with the United States; in return, they would assist us in our spiritual development. But the one condition was that we had to stop our nuclear programs, which Eisenhower refused voluntarily," Jonah explains, leaving them to ponder the implications of such a treaty.

Doyle looks over at Mike, "Is he pulling my chain?"

"No, he's not. If this is too much to comprehend, I suggest you don't go further. Wouldn't want your girly emotions shaken up," replies Mike.

Jonah walks back to the doorway, "It's okay, Doyle; you're not the first one to feel this way. There are a couple of projects that the government ran that you can read about when you have the time. Project Sigma and Project Plato. Eisenhower had another meeting in 1955 with a different group of aliens at Holloman Air Force Base in New Mexico. However, those pictures were destroyed by our government. That meeting ended with a treaty being signed, but the aliens deceived Eisenhower, and there's been trouble ever since."

The group exits the room and walks to a nearby elevator, "There's a group that played a role in the 1955 meetings that we believe was the origins of the Shadow Government. That group has been called

the Majestic Twelve," Jonah tells him, setting the stage for further revelations about these mysterious entities. He enters a code into the elevator panel, "The Majestic Twelve formed in 1947, but many believe that the group is not real; it is just a hoax to throw everyone off their scent."

After they enter the elevator, Jonah presses another button and turns to Doyle: "We've only scratched the surface, my friend. When these doors open, your life as you've known it will change forever. And remember, when I use the word 'alien, 'I'm not referring to someone from outer space, but from another dimension or realm." The anticipation of what lies beyond the doors fills the air with mystery.

Doyle doesn't respond; he stares at Jonah as he feels the elevator move downward.

"Even though they deceived Eisenhower, we gained much expertise in their advanced technology. The space program was an area in which we used their technology and in the stealth programs. And, of course, the invisible suits," Jonah tells him as they ride the elevator.

"So, all the talk about reverse technology is a fact, uh?" Doyle asks.

"And then some," replies Jonah as the elevator doors open.

Doyle sees what looks like a city with paved sidewalks. Shops run in a line on his left, while train tracks run along on the right. On the other side of the train tracks is a rock wall with windows spaced perfectly, running as far as he can see.

After they step out, he turns and looks back to his right and sees a large door opening leading to an aircraft hangar. At least fifty aircraft are lined up with maintenance technicians working on them. Seeing these advanced aircraft, such as the F-117 stealth fighter, the F-16 fighting falcon, the F-22 raptor, the SR-71 blackbird, and a U-2 dragon lady, leaves Doyle in awe.

What are those? I've never seen that before, and that looks like one of the Space Shuttles sitting in the back, Doyle thinks to himself. As he turns to follow the guys, he asks, "What are those aircraft for?"

"What aircraft?" Jonah asks him, then turns and winks at him. "Those are our means of travel, Doyle. We'll be using them for our missions."

"That's outside our purview, Doyle," Mike responds, walking up to a shop with 'SECURITY' on the door.

"Hey, Larry. How's it going?" Mike asks the man behind the counter.

"It's going terrific, Mike. Hey, Jonah, who do we have here?" Larry asks, looking at Doyle.

Jonah puts his arm around Doyle, "This is Doyle Anderson, our newest recruit."

"Holy-shit...I've heard a lot about you, Anderson. Happy to meet you, sir," he says, reaching out his hand.

"Thanks, Larry. Good to meet you too," Doyle says, shaking his hand.

Larry reaches into a drawer and pulls out a sheet of paper. He fills it out and motions for Doyle to stand behind a line on the floor. "Let's take your picture to get you a badge."

There's a flash, and then Doyle can hear a computer start processing the information. Larry walks over and picks up a round device hooked to the computer. "Okay, if you please place your right thumb here, I'll finish it."

After Doyle sticks his thumb inside, Larry closes it over his thumb. Doyle can feel small electrical shocks as he looks at Larry. The computer makes several beeping noises, and then the device pops open.

"Alrighty. Now, if you would lad, place your thumb on this scanner and look at that computer screen," Larry tells him.

Doyle walks over, places his thumb on the scanner, and notices that his picture and information have appeared on the computer monitor.

"That's your badge, your right thumb. The program compared your DNA with the DNA we have on file for you; it confirmed that it was a match. Then, it imprinted your badge under your skin. Only special readers can read it. Also, many people have asked if we implanted a chip into you, and the answer is no. We no longer need a chip to track you; we track you using your DNA signature. Unfortunately, that is outside your purview, and I cannot explain it further." The

secrecy surrounding the identification process adds a layer of suspense to the situation.

Doyle stares at his thumb, "Okay, thanks, I guess."

The door to the security office swings open. "Glad you guys made it in one piece," Leon tells them. Boy, you guys are a rough-looking bunch. Who dressed you, Jonah?" Leon asks, laughing. Jonah, a tall man with a rugged look, chuckles. "Come on, guys, let's get you some clean clothes," Leon says, holding the door open. They leave the office and notice a four-seat golf cart parked there.

"Climb on, gentlemen," Leon tells them as he climbs behind the steering wheel.

Leon starts driving after all three men are seated in the golf cart, "I'll take you guys to one of the locker rooms. Mike and Jonah have lockers there, and Doyle, I've had the guys set you one up by theirs also. There is a whole wardrobe waiting for you, Doyle."

"Sweet, thanks, brother," Doyle replies, feeling the warmth of the team's camaraderie.

They drive a short distance, making one left turn, when Leon pulls up to two large double doors. "This is it. After you guys get cleaned up, meet me over there," Leon says, pointing at an Amtrak coach car converted into a cafe.

The guys go through the doors to the locker room, and Mike motions for Doyle to follow him. "Down this way. Jonah's locker is on

the opposite side because he's a scientist," he explains, leading Doyle to a row of wooden lockers.

"Is this Mahogany wood?"

"Yes, it is. You have four lockers in this corner. Each locker has a thumb reader, so only you can open it. There are only twelve of us who use this area, you being the twelfth," Mike tells him, emphasizing the locker room's exclusivity.

"Very nice setup," replies Doyle.

"Also, all the shower stalls have benches, so you can sit down without causing that leg any more stress. Outside each shower are all the towels and soap you need. After you get dressed, you'll need to wear a lab coat and safety glasses," Mike explains, highlighting the team's thorough preparation.

Doyle opens all four lockers and notices that each has different items inside. There's one with several sets of clothing, one with personal hygiene items, one with shoes and boots, and one with lab coats and personal protective equipment. "This is very nice," he whispers to himself.

After showering and getting dressed, Doyle puts on a lab coat and safety glasses and walks back into the tunnel. He sees Mike and Jonah standing outside the cafe, waving at him. Still using his trekking pole for stability, he walks down to the cafe and enters the main entrance.

"Come on over and have a seat. This place serves the best coffee in the world," Leon says, standing up and holding his hand out.

Doyle walks over and sits down, and the other guys sit.

"Okay, guys, let me go over a few things," Leon says. "We could retrieve the other necklace device that Mike hung on a tree. One of our small drones flew in and picked it up. Our main objective was to bring you back here, Jonah; I'm glad you didn't resist that effort."

"I felt resistance was futile," Jonah replies.

"That it would have been. Second, you all eliminated one of the SG operators and one suit. That leaves them now without a functioning suit. Miller showed up with a new prototype suit, which we destroyed in the hellfire. However, we have yet to find Miller's body," Leon tells them.

"Say what?" Mike asks.

Leon frowns, "They can't find his remains. He removed the suit before it self-destructed, but there's no way he could have survived all that firepower that rained down on that mountain."

"Don't put it past that crazy bastard. I've seen him escape things that would have killed me and you," explains Doyle.

"I hear you. Anyway, the team on the mountain will continue the search through the morning and clean the site up. The team will move on if they can't find any sign of Miller."

"Is it possible that Miller had another suit to change into and escape?" asks Mike.

Leon shakes his head, "There is no other suit for him to use. The SG is out of suits; there are no more except the two we use and Jonah's old relic. No one came in to rescue him either; that airspace was shut down, with four of our teams limiting access to that location. Plus, the SG wants him taken out too...we just don't know."

Doyle leans back, "He's alive; I'll bet you money."

"Even if he is, he'll have to go into hiding with the SG looking for him. Okay, that's all I have, gentlemen. I understand they want to show you around this facility, or at least what they feel you're allowed to see, Doyle." Leon says, standing up. He shakes their hands and then turns and walks out of the cafe. He climbs on the golf cart, waves at the guys, and then drives out of sight, leaving a sense of mystery and secrecy behind.

"This coffee is amazing. Where are these beans grown?" Doyle asks.

"That's classified," Mike replies.

"Doyle, are you ready to be blown away?" Jonah asks him.

Doyle takes one last sip of the coffee, "Sure, I can't imagine you have anything else to show me that's gonna surprise me."

"Don't bet on it," snaps Mike.

"We'll go through the East wing for now, then loop back around through the North-bay to catch the northbound train at 0000 hours. It'll take us north to California City, where we both live," explains Jonah.

"Does everyone that works here live there?" asks Doyle.

Jonah stands up and walks over to a trash can. "No, about half do. The other half live in Palmdale, California. There is also a southbound train—the tracks you saw when we entered the tunnels."

"Why do you call them tunnels?" he asks Jonah.

"That's what they are. There is a spider web of them under the desert floor; they started drilling them out in the early fifties. They stretch for many miles, mostly for the trains with the bulk of the usable areas under Edwards Air Force Base. Deep enough to withstand one of those bunker-buster bombs. It's a testament to our advanced technology and ingenuity," Jonah explains, instilling a sense of awe in Doyle.

"That's crazy. How do you guys get the aircraft down here?" Doyle asks.

"Good question, Doyle. A section of the dry lake bed lowers down with the aircraft on it. It is only done at night and with our scrambler devices to keep enemy satellites from seeing," explains Jonah.

"But, that is…" Mike starts before Doyle cuts him off.

"Is outside my purview!"

Mike points at him, "Bingo!"

"So far, the area we have been in is known as our commons area. You'll find several restaurants here, plus all the locker rooms and the main hospital. PPE is not required here but is in the rest of the facili-

ty. Let's walk to the East Wing," Jonah tells them as he walks towards a check-in station.

They walk up to the checkpoint with several revolving gates, "Place your thumb in the scanner, then just walk through the gate and the metal detector," Mike says.

After they exit the metal detector, Jonah holds open a door for them to enter. Doyle sees a long tunnel with offices or rooms on both sides.

"This is the east wing. The main tunnel is one mile long and has one hundred cells or labs on each side where most of the DNA research is done, along with telepathic studies," Jonah explains as they walk down the center aisle of the main tunnel.

As they reach the halfway point of the tunnel, Doyle suddenly stops and bends over, experiencing an unexplained sensation.

"What's wrong?" Mike asks him.

"I'm not sure. I just all of a sudden felt very sick and dizzy."

"I know what it is. Hang on just a second," Jonah tells them as he walks over to one of the cells and opens the door. Doyle hears Jonah speaking in a language he has never heard, and then Jonah closes the door and returns.

"You should start to feel better now," he tells Doyle.

"How could you possibly know that?" Doyle asks as he sits on a nearby bench.

Jonah smiles, "He hit you with infrasound, my friend. I asked our associate to stop, and he agreed that he would."

"Your associate? What are you talking about?" he asks Jonah in a demanding tone.

"Oh brother, here we go," Mike sighs as he sits beside Doyle.

"Yes, one of our associates. He is from Syria, Mount Hermon to be exact," replies Jonah.

"Mount Hermon... from the Bible? That Mount Hermon?"

"That's correct," Jonah says.

"You mean his family is from there, right?"

Jonah shakes his head, "No, he is from there. And his family, too."

Doyle sits there for a few minutes until his belly stops rolling, "So, a Syrian can use infrasound, uh?"

Jonah turns and looks at him, "I never said he was a Syrian."

"Will you just tell him so we can keep moving? I'd like to get to bed before the sun comes up," snapped Mike.

"Okay, I will. The Syrian is what many would call a Nephilim or a Watcher. His ancestors descended from Heaven to Mount Hermon. He is half flesh man and half angelic being. He and his type have been in hiding for thousands of years, and we were lucky enough to convince him to work with us; in return, we guarantee his safety," Jonah explains. The Syrian possesses unique abilities, including the use of infrasound, which plays a crucial role in the unfolding mystery.

"I thought Mount Hermon was where Jesus was transfigured? Doyle asked.

"It is the same place. But it's also where the Fallen Angels touched down. I believe that's why God later used for the transfiguration of Jesus...there's something about that location we just don't understand," Jonah says as he turns away from the two guys on the bench.

"Can I meet him?" Doyle asks.

"Absolutely not. Only two of us are allowed in that room; the door I opened leads to a waiting area. The Syrian is inside another room that leads deep into the earth. If you even looked at him, you'd probably end up sick," explains Jonah.

Doyle looks at Mike, "What do you think about this?"

"I don't. Can we get moving now, please?" Mike asks Jonah.

"One last thing, Doyle. Most people that have ever seen him or the others like him call them Bigfoot. Okay, we can move along now," Jonah says, walking away.

"I'm not sure who is the craziest. Jonah, or me for listening to him," Mike tells Doyle as he gets up to follow Jonah.

Doyle laughs, "Just when I thought I've heard it all, what's next, the wolfman?"

"That's outside your purview," Jonah yells back to him.

"Of course it is," he yells.

"I've never seen him either; I think he's full of crap myself," Mike says as they speed up to catch Jonah.

"You'll notice that the tunnel narrows ahead where it connects to the north wing. We designed it so that if one of the wings ever breached, they could close off the connector hallways to secure the other wings. That way, the entire complex would not be compromised in an attack," Jonah tells them.

The narrow hallway runs for about two hundred yards and then stops at another checkpoint, except this one has four guards and two service dogs on duty.

"Gentlemen, how are we this evening?" one of the guards asks.

"We're doing great, thanks," replies Mike.

"Guys, please walk through our machines individually so we can check you out. Thanks," another guard explains.

A third guard meets them at the exit, "Okay, gentlemen, you are clear about proceeding."

The fourth guard walks up to Mike, "I'm guessing you know that you need to visit the doctor soon? Looks like you have a small amount of internal bleeding."

"First thing in the morning, Major," Mike replies.

There's a loud buzzer sound, and one of the doors to the north wing starts to open.

Jonah leads the way, then turns back to Mike and Doyle, "Right this way."

"He's enjoying this way too much," Mike whispers.

"He looks like a child in a candy store," Doyle says.

As they enter the North Wing, they notice many more people moving around working. This wing is considerably more significant than the East Wing in width and appears to have several levels. Doyle walks over to a handrail and looks down what seems to be a few hundred feet. Several disc-shaped crafts are sitting down below.

"Okay, what is this wing used for?" he asks.

Jonah and Mike walk over beside him and look down below. Jonah puts his arm around Doyle and says, "This, my friend, is the real area-51."

Doyle's gaze follows one of the disc-shaped crafts as it lifts off the floor and disappears into the night. He turns to Jonah, his eyes wide with wonder, "How do those flying machines vanish into thin air?"

Jonah laughs, "There are launch tubes that exist in many places. Some are in the desert, some are at the bottom of lakes, and some are even at the bottom of the ocean."

Mike's hand lands heavily on Doyle's back, "This is within your field, but we need to move fast if we're going to make the last train north. You're bunking at my place in California City tonight. Tomor-

row, I've got a doctor's appointment, and you've got a flight to catch. They're whisking you off to Fort Bragg to fix that leg."

Doyle turns to follow him, "Sounds good."

The three men stride purposefully towards the dimly lit train station, its platform empty and silent.

Doyle tries to understand what he saw tonight, but he soon will have no choice but to do so.

```
2345 HOURS
THIS PAST WINTER * AFTER SAR FOR JONAH
NORTH TRAIN STATION - UNDERGROUND BASE
```

"We're free to board, but the train won't set off until the stroke of zero hundred hours," Mike informs Doyle, adding a note of mystery to their journey.

The three guys board the train, and Mike leads them to an exclusive private cabin. The small cabin, reserved for a select few, boasts four luxury captains' chairs facing the middle of the room. One large window and a small bar on the wall with the door are also present.

"Why would you need a bar just going to California City? It's what, a ten-minute ride?" asks Doyle.

"This train goes all the way to Northern California. Just west of California City, it comes to the surface and uses the existing rails to the north," Mike tells him as he sits and reclines the chair back.

"It just exits out of the tunnel and into the desert?" asked Doyle.

Mike laughs, "No. A heavily armed train station is on the side of the mountain where it comes to the surface."

"I see. Does the south train come to the surface, too?"

"No, it never did. But it makes a large loop under the desert. It runs to Palmdale, east to Victorville, and back to the underground base. They wanted to add a line to Barstow, but they would have had to cross a few fault lines, so they never did. The bulk of the staff comes in from that south train, with most of the military special ops teams coming in from the north," Mike tells him.

"All aboard for the zero-hundred northbound train to Cal-City," A recorded voice comes over the intercom system, heightening the anticipation of the journey.

Doyle sees a few people heading for the train, "Not a lot of people catching the train," he says to Mike.

"No, most of the shifts run from nine to five. We only run two shifts here: 0900 to 1700 hours and then 2100 to 0500 hours. Our maintenance works from 1300 to 2100 hours and then from 0100 to 0900 hours. That's why this train runs at zero hours. It picks up maintenance personnel to get them here by 0100 hours," Mike explains.

"Interesting," Doyle says as he turns to Jonah. "Hey, you said earlier that only you and another person were allowed in that room. What did you mean by that?"

Sitting there with his eyes closed, Jonah pauses a minute before answering him. "You're a religious man, right?"

"I am...most of the time."

Before Jonah can continue, the recording blasts again, "Last call for the northbound train to Cal-City."

Once the recording stops, Jonah continues, "Well, you see. That dimension and this one cannot coexist; that is why GOD always used a burning bush or an ass to communicate with man. The suits that you have seen are not invisible because you can't see them. They are invisible to you because they enter that dimension you can not see."

"Remember the Biblical story of Belshazzar's feast when the hand appears and then writes on the wall, mene, mene, tekel, upharsin? That hand came from that dimension," Jonah explains.

Doyle nods his head, "Interesting."

"Quantum physics is just beginning to understand how all of this works. However, we have known how it works for decades, with our Watcher friend's help. I'll throw you a curve ball now; aliens are from that dimension and not outer space," he tells Doyle as he looks at him before continuing.

"For whatever reason, a tiny selection of people can interact with or even see beings from that dimension. Our associate knows that, and he can sense which of us can look at him; he's half and half - our dimension and the other," explains Jonah.

"The doors are now closing. Enjoy your trip to Cal-City," the recording says as they feel the train start to move.

"So, he only found two of you that can enter?" Doyle asks.

"No, there were six of us, but the others have since passed away. The other person, who is already ninety years old, and I are the only ones left. That's why certain people see them in the forest, and some don't," Jonah reveals, hinting at a hidden truth.

Doyle nods his head again, "I see," he says as he sits back to enjoy the short trip to California City.

"Jonah, so that you know. You'll have round-the-clock surveillance until we're certain you won't try that again," Mike tells him with his eyes closed.

"I understand, Mike."

The train pulls out of the station and heads towards its destination. The tunnel has no lighting; the only light inside the cabin is the tiny LED lights running along each bench's floor. There's nothing to see through the window, which appears to be painted black. The only way to tell that the train is moving is from the slight shakes and bumps along the trip.

"Please remain seated until the train comes to a complete stop," the recording says.

"Boy, that was fast," Doyle says.

"Twelve-minute trip is all it is," Mike replies as he flips on the overhead lights.

Jonah stands up and turns to Doyle, stretching his arm, "Doyle, it was terrific to meet and work with you. I look forward to seeing you again right here when you heal from those nasty injuries."

Doyle shakes his hand, "Jonah, it's been interesting. Yeah, I'll be back with many more questions. Maybe you'll let me meet the Syrian then."

"We'll see if he allows it," Jonah replies, then turns and walks out of the cabin.

Doyle feels the train stop as the recording continues, "Thanks for traveling with us. Please watch your step exiting the train."

"Come on, Doyle. We don't want to hold up the night shift from boarding the train," Mike tells him, handing him his bag.

Doyle grabs his bag, "Thanks. I'm right behind you."

The two guys walk down the hallway of the passenger car and then step off the train. They walk through a set of turnstiles and then up an escalator on two levels. Doyle notices a group of people waiting to get on the train during the ride up. About half wear military uniforms, while the other half wear dress suits. After they reach the top of the escalator, Mike turns right into a hallway with elevator doors that are every one hundred feet or so.

"These elevators go directly into our homes; every home in the subdivision has one as it is a gated community, and everyone that lives here works at the underground base. The US Air Force twenty-four-seven monitors this entire subdivision," explains Mike as he stops at a set of elevator doors and places his thumb into a reader. "The unique features of our homes, including the direct elevator access and the constant Air Force surveillance, make this a truly intriguing place to live."

The elevator doors open, and Mike says, "Place your thumb in the reader and then come on in."

Doyle scans his thumb and then walks into the elevator. The doors close, and a woman's voice comes over the speaker, "Welcome home, Mike. Nice to meet you, Doyle."

"Thank you, Hope. That's her name, Doyle. Say hi," Mike tells him.

"Thanks, Hope. Hi. Nice to meet you too," Doyle says to her.

The elevator takes only twenty seconds to reach Mike's basement. After it stops, the doors open, and Hope says, "I turned the heat back up to seventy degrees for you guys. Goodnight, Mike and Doyle. Sleep tight."

"Thank you. Hope, will you give me a wake-up call at 0600?" Mike asks.

"0600 it is," replies Hope.

Doyle smiles, "Thanks, Hope, goodnight."

"You can stay in the bedroom down here. Everything you need is in the bathroom over there," Mike tells him, pointing at a door on the right.

"Thanks, Mike."

"Your ride is picking you up at 0730. I'll have breakfast ready at 0645," Mike tells him, then heads up the stairs. "Oh, Leon is flying back east with you too."

"Okay, see you in the morning," replies Doyle.

He walks down a short hallway to the bedroom and flips the light switch on. He sees an empty room with just a bed, no pictures on the walls, and no other furniture. "I don't guess he's much of a decorator," he says as he drops his bag on the floor.

0645 HOURS
THIS PAST WINTER * AFTER SAR FOR JONAH
MIKE'S HOME, CALIFORNIA CITY

As Doyle reaches the top of the stairs, he can smell the bacon cooking. He follows the smell and the noise of pans clanging together to the large kitchen, where he sees Mike cooking eggs.

"Good morning. I hope you like bacon and eggs because there's plenty," Mike tells him.

"Love them, as a matter of fact," responds Doyle.

Mike dumps the eggs from the skillet into a bowl, walks over, and places the bowl on the table. He then sits another plate full of bacon

on the table and turns to Doyle: "There's decaf coffee over there, and there is milk and juice on the cart. You can't have caffeine because they may want to do surgery on you earlier in the day than planned."

"Nice, thanks, brother," Doyle says, grabbing a coffee mug and pouring him a cup.

Doyle sits at the table as Mike walks over and sits down, "Doyle, let me say grace real quick."

"Go ahead."

Mike bows his head, "...Amen."

"Amen...Silent prayer, uh?" Doyle asks him.

"That's right. You have a problem with that?" Mike asks as he reaches out, grabs a spoonful of eggs, and dumps them onto his plate.

Doyle shakes his head, "No, not at all."

"Now eat up. You don't have long before Leon will be here. You have a long trip ahead of you today, but just don't overeat. Because, like I mentioned about the surgery," Mike replies with a mouth full of eggs.

Doyle places some eggs and two pieces of bacon on his plate before the guys enjoy breakfast without talking. Just as Doyle takes his last bite, his phone vibrates.

"Looks like Leon is here," he says, standing up and shaking Mike's hand. "Mike, I appreciate everything you did for me out there; I won't soon forget it."

"Not a problem. I'm sure we will do it again soon enough," Mike replies, still sitting at the table.

Doyle turns and walks over, grabs his bag, and then walks out the front door. He sees Leon sitting in a black SUV with the window down.

"Good morning, sunshine," Leon says, then starts laughing in that familiar high-pitched laugh.

"Good morning, Leon."

"We've got a plane to catch. We're flying out of a private airstrip just a mile away. We also have a medical team onboard waiting for you," explains Leon.

"On the plane? I mean, they're going to treat me while we fly?"

Leon smiles and looks at him, "That's correct. That's how we roll dog!"

"Dog? Since when did you become hip?" Doyle asks, shaking his head.

Leon lets out another loud laugh, "You're a funny man, Doyle; damn, I've missed working with you. They'll repair your leg and knee before we touch down at Fort Bragg. Susan is already en route, and your sons will be there too."

Leon turns and looks at him, "You're one of our most important soldiers, only the best for you. Plus, we need you back up and going in a month."

Doyle looks out the window as Leon pulls out of the driveway, "What's going on in a month?"

"Doyle. You, my friend, will start looking into all these missing people in North America. We are working on a database that tracks when a person goes missing. The missing people are divided into four categories, but you will only be working on the paranormal category."

"What, like ghosts and shit?" Doyle asks, sounding agitated but excited about the mysterious and paranormal mission ahead.

Leon again laughs out loud, "No, you weirdo. Paranormal also means beyond the scope of scientific understanding. Like what you've seen with these suits and at the underground base. That's why we brought you on this search for Corey Prine, to ease you into things that most people don't know exist."

"I wondered how we found him so fast, considering we didn't have to search at all," replies Doyle.

Leon turns onto a small dirt road and pulls out onto a runway. "Our plane sits at the other end of the runway. This airstrip is inside this gated community and guarded twenty-four-seven."

"There's no air traffic control tower or hangars, uh?" asks Doyle.

"We use the tower at Edwards. Technically, this is part of Edwards Air Force base now," Leon explains as he pulls up beside the Boeing KC-767.

"I thought these planes are only used for refueling?" Doyle asks.

Leon puts the SUV in park and turns off the ignition, "They are, but this plane has been modified to be our flying hospital. However, it is still listed as an aerial refueling aircraft."

The two men exit the vehicle, and two Air Force Airmen greet them, assisting with their luggage. One of the airmen guides Doyle up the steps and into the plane. The interior is surprisingly luxurious, with spacious captain's chairs, two inviting couches, and a large monitor on the front wall. Headsets are neatly arranged on each chair. Two elegant stewardesses warmly welcome the men as they board. Halfway back, a wall and a door with a striking red cross painted on it catch Doyle's attention.

"Welcome aboard, Doyle. I've been looking forward to meeting you. I'm Captain Trogden. We flew together once after coming out of Afghanistan."

Doyle shakes his hand, "Nice to meet you, Captain. I hear that a lot, but I'm sorry I don't remember you," Doyle tells him as he shakes his hand.

"No worries, Doyle. Please follow Paige; she'll help you settle in our operating room."

Paige, standing in the back by the door to the surgical room, walks to Doyle and says, "Nice to meet you. I'm one of the nurses who will be taking care of you today."

"I kinda figured that since you're wearing scrubs," Doyle replies, then laughs softly.

She walks him to the door and then opens it. As he walks in, Doyle feels a wave of apprehension as he sees the operating table and three people standing nearby.

"Welcome, Doyle." the doctor says, putting Doyle at ease.

"Hi," responds Doyle.

"Now, I know you had a small breakfast this morning, and that's okay. We have a new way of doing things. You will not be going under but will remain awake the entire time. However, as far as you know, you will not have any clue as to what is going on around you; it'll be just like you are under. This technique is top secret, so I really can't say more. Paige will prep you for surgery, and then we'll start."

She motions for him to enter a small room to the rear, "Doyle, inside, you'll find a gown to put on. Everything else has to come off. When you're ready, just press the button on the wall inside."

"Yes, ma'am."

Doyle enters the room, leans his trekking pole in the corner, and undresses. He puts the gown on and then removes his underwear. "Damn, I hate people cutting on me," he says as he reaches up and presses the button, then sees a mist coming out of a vent on the ceiling before everything goes black.

1600 HOURS
THIS PAST WINTER * AFTER SAR FOR JONAH
FORT BRAGG, NORTH CAROLINA

"Hi, sweetie. I've missed you," Susan says to Doyle, reaching out and grabbing his hand.

Doyle looks around and sees he's lying in a bed with an IV in his left arm. "Where am I?"

"We're in the Womack Army Medical Center at Fort Bragg," she tells him.

Doyle rubs his head, "I don't remember anything about the flight or the surgery. What time is it?" he asks her.

Susan looks at her watch, "It is four-fifteen pm Eastern time."

"I lost over eight hours. Well, just five hours if you count the time change," Doyle replies, sitting in bed.

"Don't try and get up; the doctor said he'll be in here by four-thirty."

Doyle lays back down, then reaches down and feels his leg, "It's not a very big brace they put on me."

"Don't mess with it, honey," she says, pulling his hand away from his leg.

"Where are the boys?" he asks her.

"They will meet us tonight for dinner," she replies as the doctor walks into the room.

"How are you feeling, Mr. Anderson?" the doctor asks.

"I'm feeling pretty good, just a little tired."

"That's to be expected, Doyle. You'll be happy that your knee only had a few bone chips. We cleaned that up and placed a small pin in your Tibia to help heal. Fortunately, the break was a stable fracture, so it was still aligned correctly."

"The knee will start feeling better in a few weeks; the leg, however, will take six to eight weeks. Stay off it for the first two weeks, and then I want to see you again here. If all looks well, we'll start you on a therapy schedule," the doctor explains.

Doyle reaches up and shakes the doctor's hand, "Thanks, Doc."

"You dodged a huge bullet; it could have been worse if you'd landed on it a few inches lower."

"I guess I got lucky, Doc."

"Well, from what I hear about you, you're almost bulletproof," the doctor tells him as he walks towards the door. You guys are free to head home. A nurse will be in here soon with a wheelchair to help you. If you need anything, just let my office know," the doctor tells them, then disappears out the door.

Susan grabs a bag and sits it on the bed, "I brought you a change of clothes, babe."

"Thanks, honey," he replies just as the phone rings.

He looks over at Susan, shrugs his shoulders, and then picks up the phone, "Maybe it's the nurse."

He places the phone to his ear when a loud, high-pitched whistle makes him drop it. "Oh my goodness," he says, rubbing his ear and picking up the phone.

"Hello," he says.

There's a slight silence before a voice whispers, "Hey buddy."

"Who is this?" Doyle asks.

"Come on, Anderson, are you really this dumb?"

"Miller?"

"That's correct."

"How...did you..." Doyle starts to say before Miller cuts him off.

"Do you and Susan still call people you are searching for Manglers?"

"Yeah...why?" he asks Miller.

"As soon as I'm finished dealing with the Senator, I'm coming for you, Anderson! I am the Mangler now!"

Doyle looks at Susan as the phone call disconnects.

"That was Miller?" she asks.

"It was...I guess."

Doyle turns and looks out the window. The sun starts to set as the sky turns a pale shade of orange with dark lines stretched across the winter canvas. "I will have to start at Miller's last known position..."

MANGLER
BOOK III

POINT LAST SEEN

Don't be afraid to get lost, because that's where the adventures begin.

Unknown

CHAPTER ONE
MILLERS LAST KNOWN POSITION

1630 HOURS
TWO MONTHS AFTER DOYLES HOSPITAL'S RELEASE * PRES-
ENT-DAY
THE DEVIL'S BATHTUB, CALIFORNIA * SITE OF COL.
MILLER'S DEMISE

As the sun dips below the horizon, casting long shadows over the rugged landscape, Doyle and his small team conclude their arduous four-day expedition. Doyle, still using a cane from the ass beating that Miller gave him on that horrific night, walked over to Harold, the ex-Green-Beret. "Please tell me you found something, anything?" Even though Doyle already knows that Harold couldn't possibly find much after the intensive steps the Shadow Government takes to hide their presence. But Harold is the best tracker in the business.

"Doyle, I wish I had more to give you than I have. There is no question that Colonel Miller never left this position......on foot anyway. Based on the equipment he reportedly wore, this area is indeed his

last known position." Harold replied, pointing to a charred spot on the side of the mountain. Harold came here reluctantly, fearing that Doyle might be overstepping his boundaries and that the possibility of a Shadow Government trap was genuine.

Doyle pulled the hood of his jacket up over his head. The temperature was well below freezing at this altitude, and the wind was picking up now that the sun had set. Harold patted him on the back, "We are lucky that this has been a snow-free winter to this point, or we would not have been able to land the helicopter this close." The Patriot's Group would never fund this operation for fear of putting Doyle in harm's way. Doyle was in Bakersfield, Califonia, for a search and rescue conference and flew Harold in to help look for clues on Miller's disappearance.

"That is true. There is no way I could have climbed up here with this cane." Doyle turned to look Harold in the eyes, "I'm telling you that it was Miller on that phone, no doubt about it." While in the hospital for his leg surgery, Doyle received a call from Colonel Miller.

"I believe that you feel it was Colonel Miller, but the facts lead me to believe that he is dead. They are getting very good at using AI to trick people." After Harold tells him this, he walks over to the kill site and turns back to Doyle. "There is just no way a person could have survived this." The area has nothing remaining; there are no trees, brush, and even several boulders turned to powder from the fire-fight that took place here.

Doyle smiled, "I didn't say he survived. I'm saying somehow he figured out how to transform into another dimension." Doyle watched closely at Harold's face as those words fell on him.

"What are you saying, Doyle? That he didn't die and now is stuck in limbo?"

"Come on, Harold, don't give me that crap. You damn well know what I am talking about. Didn't your Indian elders believe in other dimensions? What were they called......you know what I'm trying to say...Skinwalkers! That's it. Are they not other-dimensional creatures?"

Harold laughed, "People do not become Skinwalkers after they die. You are confusing two different things, my friend. Skinwalkers never walked this earth as a flesh man. However, I think I know what you are trying to say about that new type of suit he was wearing. But for us to say or even think that man has found a way to jump dimensions is not something I'm willing to say. That new suit just gives the operator a better type of invisibility, that is it."

Even as Harold says it is impossible, he knows the military has always tried to build a suit that would hop from dimension to dimension. But, he is not willing to believe they accomplished this.

"Harold, you are the smartest man I know in both the ways of man and God, but I'm sorry you are wrong about this. All I'm asking of you is to believe that Miller called me. I'm telling you that without a doubt in my mind, I just need you to help me figure out a way to

stop him from doing any more evil." Doyle knows that might be impossible.

"Doyle, as promised to your dad, I am always willing to help. However, it will take me some time and a lot of work to come up with answers for you. We cannot completely stop evil works; we can only slow them down. There will be five new Colonel Millers that will fill that void left by his death. But I will do my best."

"That is all I ask of you," before Doyle could say another word, the helicopter pilot approached with a concerned look.

"Guys, we should probably get going, like now. There is a crazy storm that just popped up on the radar, and the winds are not something we should try to fly in on this mountain."

"Thanks, Peterson. Give us a minute to grab our gear," Doyle replied.

"I'll help you and Harold; we have little time. I've never seen a storm come on so quickly," Peterson told Doyle. He has flown Doyle out of many tight spots in Afghanistan and Iraq and one winter storm in upstate New York.

Harold looked to the sky and deeply breathed, "Man has figured out a way to manipulate the weather. I feel someone wants us off this mountain." He had seen storms pop up out of nowhere searching for lost people and could tell by the smell if it was Mother Nature's or man's doing.

The wind blew Doyle's hood from his head and almost made him lose his balance, "You believe man can change the weather, Harold, but you do not believe what I was saying about dimensions!" he shouted over the wind.

The three guys rounded up all the gear as the wind began to beat down off the mountaintop to the north. Doyle headed to the helicopter first since he moved at half the speed of the others. Harold squatted down at the kill site and used his knife to scrap some of the debris off the rocks into a small bag. He closed his eyes and started chanting something in a low voice. Peterson put the last gear into the helicopter and helped Doyle get strapped in.

"Come on, Harold. We must get off the ground, or we will spend another night on this mountain!" Peterson yelled as he started the helicopter. Harold ran over and climbed inside.

As the aircraft lifted off the ground, Doyle grabbed his phone to text Susan that they were in the air and heading back in. He watched as the site below slowly disappeared from his vision and thought about Amy Leek, Jonah's sister who died on this mountain that same night as Colonel Miller. I wonder if Jonah knew it was his sister who came to kill us, he thought.

"Hang on, guys, it's going to be a bumpy ride to the airfield outside Mesa, California," Peterson told them as he fought the stick on the helicopter. Susan awaits them there with the small jet they rented for

this trip. Peterson is also the pilot of that aircraft. "Just get us there in one piece, brother," Doyle shouted.

```
1200 HOURS
TWO MONTHS EARLIER
UNDISCLOSED LOCATION, WASHINGTON DC
```

Secret service agents lined the hallway to the SCIF (Sensitive compartmented information facility) as the United States Vice President walked with a cup of coffee. One of the agents took the Vice President's raincoat from him. It has been raining for six straight days in the capital. Tensions are thick in the air due to the word getting out that Colonel Miller stole one of the new top-secret invisible suits and killed several agents before destroying the new suit.

"I'm in no mood for any bullshit," the Vice President said just after the SCIF door closed. "I want to know how Colonel Miller got his hands on that suit, and I want to know all about Sergent Anderson." He had spent the last few hours reading about Doyle Anderson's career in the military.

"Sir. We can't begin until Senator Douglas arrives," one of the agents replied. Senator Douglas is the commander of the Shadow Government's ground forces.

"Senator Douglas has been relieved of his duties. I am in the process of naming a successor. Do you have any questions?" The Vice President looked at every face in the room, looking for any sign of weakness.

"Sir, are you worried about what the President might find out?" one of the military officers asked as he handed him the report on Colonel Miller.

"Not at all. That damn fool is more concerned about re-election than caring what we are doing with our military equipment. Now, tell me about Anderson."

In the meeting, the highest-ranking Navy officer slid the Vice President a folder and began, "Sir. Doyle Anderson is a highly deco-rated combat veteran—an Army Ranger out of Fort Bragg. Anderson served in multiple combat missions in Iraq, two in Afghanistan, and even a top-secret combat mission in South Africa. He taught many of our best Army Rangers and has held some of the highest security clearances. After he chose not to re-enlist, he was re-deployed into combat for a final mission with a contractor unit. That re-deployment mission is the one we used one of our operators to bring down a CH-47 Chinook helicopter, the payback we owed the enemy. Sergent Anderson's best friend was on that helo, Sir."

The Vice President reviewed the file, "I understand he has been doing Mountain search and rescue for the past few years. So, how did he cross paths with us again, Admiral?"

"Sir, Senator Douglas was running a mission in the Smokie Moun-tains, where he was putting pressure on one of our weapons engi-neers, Mr. Wolfgang."

After slamming his fist on the table, the Vice President interrupted the Admiral, "Senator Douglas was not just putting pressure on him; he murdered his son. This committee and I should have cleared that. Hang on just a second, Admiral." He turned to one of the CIA agents in the meeting. "Senator Douglas will return to his ranch in Wisconsin soon but will not leave that place alive. Understood?"

"Yes, Sir. Understood."

"Admiral, please continue."

"Thank you, Mr. Vice President. That is correct that Anderson had moved into search and rescue. He was called in to search for the young Wolfgang kid. While searching for this boy, he ran into the operator that the Senator chose to use. Colonel Miller."

"Colonel Miller, as I understand it, came up through the ranks with Anderson. And for some damn reason, Senator Douglas decided to use Colonel Miller on a mission where he and Anderson could potentially run into each other. Which they did, and Colonel Miller allowed Anderson to see one of our combat invisibility suits," the Vice President scoffed. "Does that cover what happened accurately, Admiral?"

"Yes, Sir. That is correct. Colonel Miller thought it would be enough to halt the search for the Wolfgang kid by allowing Anderson to see one of the suits, but this was false, Mr. Vice President."

"It wasn't false; it was ignorant and led Anderson right to the boy and then into General X's Patriots group. Yes, Admiral, I know about

Anderson joining that group. That is why I sent our kill group to eliminate Colonel Miller in California." General X is the man many believe formed the Patriot's Group decades ago, although he is listed as dead now. "I'll recap, gentlemen, Anderson and Miller came up together, we killed Anderson's best friend, and then Miller showed Anderson the top-secret suit we killed his friend with. Should I add another turd to this shit pile?" the Vice President asked as he tossed the file onto the table.

"Unfortunately, Yes, Sir. One other individual saw the suit, Anderson's childhood friend, Louis Lee. He is now in protective custody within the Patriot's group. Senator Douglas sent a hit squad to kill him, but that too failed…Sir." the admiral replied.

The Vice President rubbed his chin, "How did that fail? Let me guess, Doyle Anderson?"

"That is correct, Sir. He arrived at the hit site and forced the hitmen away from Mr. Lee. He then was able to save Mr. Lee's life…Sir," the Admiral replied.

The room remained quiet for some time as the Vice President sat and rubbed his chin before he spoke, "As I understand it, Anderson was then used in California to rescue the Physicist Mr. Prine, or Jonah as he goes by these days. Jonah had worked for both our group and General X's. He was hiding up on that mountain when his sister, Amy Leek, was killed." The Vice President turned and looked at Chuck Leek, "Your now deceased wife."

"That is correct. We sent Amy up the mountain to kill Jonah and Anderson in one of our suits. As it turned out, their number three guy, retired Marine Sergeant Major Mike Rosen, killed her before she could complete the mission," Chuck replied.

The Vice President nodded, "As most of you know, Chuck and Mike worked together in our group before Mike betrayed us and joined General X's group. Chuck, I have good news for you. You are going to one of our secret locations in Wisconsin, where you will wait until Senator Douglas returns to his ranch there. We will make sure Anderson comes to that ranch to confront the Senator; then, you will kill them both. You then will take over the Senator's business in running our sex trafficking operation. Understood?"

"It would be my pleasure to remove the Senator," Chuck said, making notes in his planner. Chuck had been the Shadow government hitman for years. He was a real gangster-type man; this is the reason Mike left the group, for he didn't believe in cold-blooded murder. However, if there was cause, Mike was one of the best hitmen himself.

"Who knows, Chuck? Maybe you'll get lucky, and Mike will show up with Anderson. If that happens, you also have the approval of this committee to remove Mike," the Vice President told him.

Chuck smiled, "This just keeps getting better. Thank you, sir."

The door to the SCIF slowly opens, and a scent of smoke fills the room as two guards dressed entirely in red enter. A tall man enters the room wearing a fine white suit; a small crown sits atop his head, and

his snow-white hair and long beard hang to his waist, following the guards into the SCIF. He carried a walking cane with a silver dragon's head as the handle. The men sitting around the table all stand and bow. "Gentlemen, your leader of the Shadow Government, the honorable Dr. Furcus, is in your presence," one of the guards shouts.

"You may be seated, my disciples," Dr. Furcus told them. "I have been briefed on the events surrounding Colonel Miller and thought it would be best if I flew here today from my compound in Antarctica. I have meditated with my master, and we have decided that the time to act is upon us." Dr. Furcus walked to the far side of the SCIF floatingly; no movement from his legs was visible to the men in the room. He spoke with his face towards the wall, "Just as Pontius Pilate tried to interfere with our business, we shall not let this Doyle Anderson do the same!"

After Dr. Furcus raised his voice, the SCIF went dark and vibrated viciously. The lights flickered on and off for thirty seconds. When the lights finally came back on, Dr. Furcus sat on a throne at the head of the table that was not in the SCIF prior. The two red guards stood at attention on each side of the throne. Dr. Furcus's eyes were solid black, and his pupils were small red dots. In Ancient Aramaic, he mumbled that he looked each man in the eyes individually. When his gaze was upon the Vice President, Dr. Furcus's eyes returned to a beautiful white and blue.

"Mr. Vice President, you were chosen by me and my leader to serve in this role to install the one-world system and return my master to

his rightful throne. You have done a remarkable job installing our one-world system in North America. Although, the people you hand-picked have not lived up to the standards we have set." Dr. Furcus turned to the others, "As you, gentleman, know, you gave your soul to us to achieve wealth and power. You chose not to be actors or musicians but to be politicians. Some of you hide within the military as officers or even as part of the Intelligent Agency. But no doubt about it, you all are politicians. We own your soul in this life and the next."

"Dr. Furcus, I assure you that this little problem with Colonel Miller and Doyle Anderson will be corrected very soon by myself and my top hitman," the Vice president told him.

Dr. Furcus smiled, "That is why I traveled here today. This Anderson comes in the spirit of Elijah to destroy my Jezebel once again. I will not allow that this time. First, no one within this group will touch Senator Douglas. I chose him, and I will decide when to remove him. Second, any weak links must go. Now, about your so-called top hitman, would that be Chuck Leek?" he asked, turning to face Chuck.

"Yes, Sir. That is he, Mr. Leek."

"I understand, Mr. Vice President. You will be shocked that Mr. Leek has played both sides, with us and the Patriot's group. He is the one who allowed Colonel Miller to steal our latest invisibility suit or, to explain it correctly, our new multi-dimensional suit. He had asked Colonel Miller to kill his wife after she killed Jonah and Anderson."

"That's bullshit, Mr. Vice President," Chuck shouted.

"Guards, secure Mr. Leek," Dr. Furcus ordered. How dare you speak without permission. You are no more than dirt under my foot, for our group has spent over two thousand years waiting for the opportunity to arise again. Guards, dispose of Mr. Leek so the dogs can eat him."

The two red guards walked over to Chuck Leek. "What's going on, Mr. Vice President?" Chuck asked as he stood up between the two guards. One of the guards grabbed Chuck by the arm, and suddenly, the other guard put a plastic bag over Chuck's head and zipped-tied it tight around his neck. The guards dragged him and his chair to one of the SCIF's corners and sat him in the chair. One removed a roll of duct tape from his inner jacket pocket, and they taped Chuck to the chair as he kicked.

Chuck kicked and jerked as the bag fogged up before he went still. The men in the SCIF sat quietly until the Vice President broke the silence. "Dr. Furcus, we will fix this and make you proud of us again."

The two red guards returned to Dr. Furcus's side. "Mr. Vice President, I hope so for your sake. Do not make me come here again, for if I do, I will find the tallest tower in this city and have you thrown off of it." After Dr. Furcus spoke this, the SCIF went dark, and the sound of a thousand screaming voices filled the air. When the SCIF lit back up, Dr. Furcus and his two red guards, along with Chuck Leek's body,

were gone. The men in the room sat with their hands covering their ears. The Vice President slowly stood.

"That concludes our meeting today, gentleman. None of this leaves this room, understood? The nine remaining of us, as Dr. Furcus said, are the front line for installing the one-world system in North America and returning Ba'al to his rightful seat." The Vice President exited the SCIF. The remaining eight men locked hands and started a low chant as the SCIF door closed.

The Vice President pulled his phone from a secure box outside the SCIF. He scrolled through his contacts and then pressed the call button. "Senator Douglas, where are you at? Oh, you are already at the restaurant? I will be canceling our meeting this afternoon, Senator. That is correct. You are one lucky bastard! Even though I cannot fire you right now, I can make your life a living hell. No, you kiss my ass, Senator! Goodbye now." The vice President slams his phone onto the floor, shattering it. He turns to one of his security guards, "Where the hell is my car?"

Senator Douglas stared at his phone, smiling.

The Vice President's SUV pulled away from the secret location.

Dr. Furcus and his red guards boarded a private jet back to Antarctica.

Chuck Leek's body floats in the Potomac River.

Ex-Governor of California, Chuck Leek, dies of apparent suicide in Washington, DC. It will be the front page story nationwide in the morning.

INTERLUDE

JONAH

A video screen of a significant size changes from blank to a view of seven distinct gentlemen, each with unique features and expressions, sitting at a table. They each have a keypad in front of them for this crucial meeting.

These gentlemen look concerned but with great determination. I dislike these meetings, but General **X** wants us to do this.

"Good morning, gentlemen," I say to them, my voice firm and my mind focused on the tasks ahead, not wasting my time with these guys.

"Doyle Anderson, our recruit, is recovering from leg and knee surgery and has returned to his home in the enigmatic North Carolina mountains. I will give him a month to rest and spend time with his wife, Susan before I send him a new assignment."

Look at them, all seven just staring into the camera, occasionally looking at one another and me before one of them types on his keypad.

It's been eighteen months since our last briefing. Let's catch up on the crucial developments of our mission.

"Yes, of course. Last September, during a search and rescue mission in the Great Smoky Mountains for the young boy Allen Wolfgang, Doyle Anderson, the lead searcher, encountered one of the Shadow Government's top-secret invisible suits. Mr. Anderson had always been on our shortlist for bringing on to our group, and I believe Colonel Miller arranged for Anderson to see the suit, hoping to recruit him for the Shadow Government.

Mr. Anderson found the Wolfgang boy, and we saved his life. However, Mr. Anderson's best friend also saw the suit and was put on a hitlist by the shadow Government, and we have him in protective custody as we speak.

This past winter, we brought Mr. Anderson to California to search for me, hoping that he would lure Colonel Miller in and allow us to deal with him once and for all. And that mission is where Mr. Anderson sustained his injury."

That should keep them guessing for a while.

The Shadow Government will try and eliminate Mr. Anderson.

"Yes, I agree with your assessment; the Shadow Government will send their hitmen against Doyle. I will send one of my robotic owls

to his location, and it will monitor his every move. My owls have enough firepower to take out a small army. Still, I will also have a guard with an invisible suit within striking distance of Doyle's location until he recovers from the surgeries, and then I'll just keep the owl nearby."

Are you not worried about Doyle's PTSD?

What, are you kidding me? Of course, I'm worried about Doyle, but I won't tell you that.

"No, I am not worried about Doyle's handicap. As you gentlemen know, we have had our best luck using recruits with underlying illnesses or handicaps. The Shadow Government also targets these individuals for their enhanced ability to interact with dimensional entities." That should keep their thoughts busy for a while.

Lightning flashes outside, illuminating the dark room. Man, that was a good one.

"These bad weather events are escalating, which means we have the Shadow Government on their heels. Don't you guys agree?" Okay, you all just look at one another again while I sit in this electrical storm; now, look at me so I can read your message.

Is that average weather there?

"No, this part of California normally doesn't experience thunderstorms like this, a highly unusual and unsettling phenomenon. A sign of the escalating danger we face."

Another building-rattling clap of thunder shakes the small church.

I must hurry this conversation before one of those lightning bolts hits my satellite while in service.

"I am working on arranging to have Doyle in the Crazy Mountains in Montana shortly. The local legend has many stories about the witch of the Crazy Mountains, and if they are correct, she should appear again very soon, and people will go missing. I want Doyle to put an end to her reign of terror."

What is he typing?

What is the status of Colonel Miller? Has he been removed?

I wondered when they were going to ask about him.

"Colonel Miller's status? When we hit him with that missile, the latest invisibility suit he wore allowed him to go from this dimension to the unseen one. I have not confirmed this as of yet. But Doyle did receive a phone call from him afterward. He could not have survived that hellfire without slipping out of the known dimension."

The seven men huddle with their backs turned away from the camera, their actions shrouded in secrecy. The thunderstorm continues, shaking Jonah's small church as the video screen flickers. The men turn back to face Jonah, their faces unreadable, their intentions unknown.

We think it's time to introduce Mr. Anderson to General X.

"Yes, sir, I will help arrange for General **X** to meet with Doyle. A large cold front will approach North America from the west; I will use that front as cover to move General **X** from our headquarters on the other side of the ice wall beyond Antarctica to Washington DC."

Thank you, Jonah. We are ending transmission.

"Thank you, gentlemen."

"I'll have to wait this storm out before returning to my Edwards Air Force Base office," Jonah said, leaning back in his chair and watching the lightning flash.

CHAPTER TWO

FIGMENT OF IMAGINATION

The April sun is starting to appear on the horizon as the sky turns a deep, fiery orange. The clouds from the rain overnight have long drifted away as a cool spring morning dawns. A lost little girl awakened from her sleep underneath several downed trees. She heard dogs barking off in the distance as she squinted in the bright sunlight, peeking out from her hiding spot. The sun blinded her briefly as she noticed what looked like legs walking toward her location. Fearing it was a witch who lived in the mountains, she crouched down, hoping the witch would not see her. The little girl placed her hand in front of her face to block the bright early morning sunlight and then noticed that the person had stopped. She watched intently as the person squatted down and removed a camouflaged hat from their head.

"Hello, Bella. I'm Doyle. Everyone has been looking all night for you."

"Go away!" She yelled back to him, still holding her hands over her eyes.

"It's okay, honey. I'm helping your mom and dad find you and take you home."

"I'm not supposed to talk to strangers," she snapped.

Doyle sat down and situated himself where he blocked the sun from her eyes. He removed his backpack, reached in, and pulled out a water bottle. "Would you like a drink, Bella?"

"No!" she snapped as she pushed further under the tree away from him.

Doyle whistled and then shouted, "Come on, Gunner! Heir! (German for come/here). Would you like to meet my dog?"

Bella looked up at him, "Maybe. Is he a nice dog?" she asked.

Gunner ran out of the bush and up to Doyle as he rubbed his back, saying, "Yes, he is very nice. Especially to little girls."

Bella looked at Gunner and smiled, then hid her face again.

"Gib Laut (German for speak)," Doyle told Gunner.

Gunner turned his head to the left and barked several times. Bella raised her head and smiled. "He wants you to talk to him."

She slowly crawled out of her hiding spot and stood staring at Gunner. Doyle noticed she had no shoes and was missing her pants, wearing only a tee-shirt and a pull-up. "Sweetie, where did your shoes go?" he asked her.

"The bear took them," she replied, reaching out and patting Gunner on his head.

"Sitz (German for sit)," Doyle said to Gunner. "What bear took your shoes?"

Bella laughed as Gunner licked her hand. "You know, the big brown one that was keeping me safe from the witch."

Doyle looked around towards Huggins Ridge, "Where is the bear now, Bella?"

Bella pointed to the west, "She said it was her bedtime and went to the cave. She stayed with me all night and kept me warm. She sang to me just like mommy do."

"Did you two stay under this tree last night?" Doyle asked.

"No. We stayed in the cave."

"The cave she is in now?" asked Doyle.

"No, silly. The cave with the other bears. Far away," replied Bella, rubbing Gunners back.

Doyle stood up, then asked, "How did you get here, under this tree?"

"The bear said it was time for me to go home."

Doyle looked around the area, then asked. "Did you walk here?"

"No, Silly. I rode on her back just like I do with Daddy at home," she replied.

"Okay. Well, we better get going so you can see your mom and dad," he said to her. "My friend is coming with your parents, and we need to get to the trail to meet them."

Doyle clips Gunner onto his leash and grabs his radio, "Come in, Scotty." Scotty is the young man who helped Doyle search for the Wolfgang boy.

"Yeah, go ahead, Doyle."

"Scotty, I found her. We are just north of Bear Creek Trail, just before where it comes to an end. We are about one hundred yards up the ridge, near several downed trees."

"That's great news! We are very close to there now, Doyle. I'll come up and meet you guys."

"Roger-that," Doyle replied, then turned to Bella. "Your mom and dad are just down below. Do you want me to carry you down the slope, sweetie?"

"Yes, please," Bella replied, still rubbing Gunner.

Doyle hooked Gunner's leash to his belt, then reached down and picked up Bella. He eased down the slope, mindful of placing his feet due to the early morning dew casing the ground and rocks as the birds called to one another. Gunner started whining when he saw Scotty coming toward their location.

"I'll tell you one thing, Doyle. For a guy with one good leg, you sure do move around these mountains great," Scotty said, walking up to them.

Doyle smiled, "What can I say? I guess I have good genes."

"You have something for sure. By the way, it was a great call looking on this ridge for her," Scotty replied, shaking his head. "I can't believe she made it this far."

"Never underestimate lost people in the forest, even if the lost person is only three years old. Isn't that right, Bella?" Doyle asked her as he rubbed the top of her head before he put her down.

"The bear showed me the way," she replied

Scotty looked at Doyle, "What bear?"

"That is what I'm going to find out. Bella said it went into a cave. There is one off to the west, and she pointed in that direction," Doyle said. Then he leaned down to Bella and took her hand. "Bella, Scotty is going to take you the rest of the way to meet your mom, okay?"

"Okay," she whispered.

"Say bye to Gunner," said Doyle, handing her hand to Scotty.

Now in Scotty's arms, she waved and yelled, "Bye, Gunner!"

Doyle and Gunner watched them until they went out of sight, and then they heard Bella's mom crying when she saw her daughter. "Oh, my baby! I'm so happy you are okay."

"What do you say, buddy? You want to go find this bear?" Doyle asked Gunner, squatting down beside him and rubbing his side.

Doyle unclipped him from his leash, and the two climbed back up the ridge to look for the bear. The sun had fully risen above the horizon, and most of the mountain wildlife was engaged in their daily activities as they reached the point of the downed trees.

Gunner looked up at him and barked. "Yeah, she is safe now," Doyle continued walking, patting himself on the hip, which triggered Gunner to follow. They hiked over the west side of Huggins Ridge, then turned to the north-west, "I remember there being a small cave not far from here,"

The west side of the ridge could be brighter, with the mountain blocking most of the sun. The ground was still very damp with dew as they strode along. Finally, Doyle stopped to get his bearings.

"I believe it is just past that ridge over there," he said, pointing to a small rocky ridge a few hundred yards away. But before they continued, an owl hooting echoed through the valley below.

Doyle looked in that direction and said softly, "I'll always think of Jonah's owl when I hear that."

He continued across the ridge to the area where the cave was located. Gunner followed close behind on the narrow trail as Doyle used his trekking pole to keep from slipping over the edge. The smell of rotten flesh smacked Doyle in the face as he rounded the bluff. Finally reaching the cave, he stopped, jammed his trekking pole in

the ground, and removed his 9mm from its holster. "Bleib (German for stay)," Doyle said to Gunner, holding his left hand up. He slowly moved forward, his gun in his right hand, as he saw the cave entrance covered with vines and moss.

Doyle felt that familiar tingling in his forearms as his adrenaline started pumping like a drag car driver seeing the Christmas tree lights counting down. His vision now became super clear as time slowed to a crawl. Then, while controlling his breathing, just like an old Navy Seal buddy taught him back in the day, he saw what was causing the stench.

He entered the cave, stepping over a dead deer carcass, then removed his flashlight from his pocket to inspect the small cave. "Nothing," he said out loud, shining the light around inside. "Heir (German for here)," he yelled to Gunner as he exited the cave, walking to retrieve his trekking pole. He turned back and leaned down to inspect the deer, "There are no signs that a bear or any animal killed this. If a bear was staying in this cave, why hasn't it eaten this thing?" he asked, looking at Gunner.

"There are no other caves in this area that I'm aware of, buddy," he said, patting Gunner on his head. "There are no signs anything has been bedding down here...strange. Why has this deer laid here and rotted without scavengers consuming it?"

Doyle walked to the bluff's edge, looked around, and noticed no animals were moving around. "I'm not liking what I see," he said out

loud. Then, he saw movement out of the corner of his right eye. Slowly turning his head, it came into clear view—the most unique-looking white owl sitting on a branch. Taking steady, slow steps, he moved closer to the owl. "Hey there."

Doyle jumped as he felt a vibration in his chest pocket. "Damn phone. Scared the crap out of me," he mumbled, pulling the phone out and squinting to see the text in the bright morning sunlight before reading it.

Doyle, don't harass my owl. I thought I would check in on you to see how the leg is doing. Regards, Jonah.

He looked back at the owl just as it flew off to the northeast, then tried to reply to the text.

That's odd. I can't reply to this text, Doyle thought, inspecting the text.

"Heir," he said to Gunner. "Doesn't look like there's anything to the bear story. Plus, I'm ready for breakfast at Sally's Diner. How about you?" Gunner barked twice in response.

Doyle and Gunner turned and headed for Bear Creek trail, the only well-worn trail in the area. The two have been in the mountains all night in the pouring rain, searching for Bella after she wandered off from her parents' campsite in the Deep Creek campgrounds near Bryson City, North Carolina. As they reached the trail, they saw Scotty sitting on a four-wheeler.

"You two want a ride to your truck?" Scotty asked.

Doyle smiled, "Absolutely."

"Where'd you park, Doyle?"

"I parked by the Road to Nowhere Tunnel," Doyle told him.

"Oh. Okay. That's not very far at all. Boy, you focused right in on that little girl. How did you know to start from there?"

"I had figured Bella was heading west and wanted to get ahead of her. However, upon finding her tracks, I knew she had moved further west than I anticipated. I followed this trail until I heard her singing and followed the sound."

"It is just unbelievable the feeling you have for lost people, Doyle," Scotty said, starting the four-wheeler. "Climb on, fellas."

Doyle climbed on the back of the four-wheeler, facing backward, holding Gunner in his lap. "Hang on, buddy," he said as Scotty gave the four-wheeler gas.

They slowly started down the narrow trail that winds along the ridges and past the backcountry campsite number 75. Then, they continued onto the path that led to the Road to Nowhere Tunnel.

"The government built this tunnel in the 1940s to replace the old road beneath Fontana Lake. When the government flooded this area, they promised to create a new road to access family cemeteries. They made it past this tunnel before environmental issues caused delays." Doyle explained, then continued. "They ultimately decided it was too

expensive to complete, and the locals gave it the Road to Nowhere name."

"That is crazy. This tunnel always gives me the creeps," Scotty replied as they pulled up beside Doyle's truck.

Doyle looked at him, "I could tell you stories about this tunnel that would keep you up at night, but that'll have to wait until next time."

"I can't wait," replied Scotty, then asked, "Where's your new truck?"

"I haven't got used to driving it yet; besides, me and this old truck go a long way back," he replied, patting the truck's hood.

"Boo!" Susan yelled, jumping out from behind the truck.

"What in the world are you doing up here, girl?" Doyle asked, jumping back.

"I thought I would go for a bike ride and see how you were doing. But I already know because I saw the rescue team load the little girl in an ambulance."

"Yeah, we found her just after sunrise," replied Doyle, moving her bike over and laying his backpack in the truck's bed.

"Hello, Susan... Doyle, I'm going to head back to base camp. Talk to you later," Scotty said and then drove off.

"Later, Scotty," Doyle said, then turned to Susan. Are you hungry, babe?"

"I'm always hungry," she replied, laughing.

"I'm going to Sally's. Is that okay with you?"

Susan hugged Doyle, "That is fine, as long as I'm with you, babe."

After hugging her, he opened the truck's back door and patted the seat. Gunner ran over and jumped in.

"Dad is meeting us there. He texted me last night, saying he had something important he wanted to talk about over breakfast."

"Barry always has something he wants to discuss during breakfast," she replied, climbing into the truck.

Doyle opened the driver's door, "That's for sure."

As they pulled out of the trailhead parking area, Doyle saw that owl sitting in a tree nearby. "Crazy old man," he said, pointing at the owl.

"Oh my. That is one pretty owl," Susan said, pulling her phone out to take a picture.

"That's one of Jonah's robot owls. Don't take a picture of it, babe."

She looked at him, "Really? What is it doing here?"

Doyle shook his head, "I have no clue. Spying on me, I guess."

They laughed, drove off as the owl watched, and slowly disappeared.

0922 HOURS
PRESENT-DAY
SALLY'S DINER, BRYSON CITY, NORTH CAROLINA

Doyle cracked the truck windows for Gunner. "I'll bring you back some food, buddy," he said as he and Susan walked towards the diner's door.

"Doyle, Susan. Over here," Barry said, holding up his arm.

"A small diner like this, and Dad thinks we won't see him," Doyle said to Susan, laughing.

"You hush. You'll be your dad's age one day, Doyle."

Barry stood up, "You two have a seat. I heard you found the girl, Doyle?"

"We did, Dad."

"Good job, son. You have a gift for finding people in distress. But, listen, the reason I wanted to meet you for breakfast is this," Barry said, laying a small leather-bound journal on the table.

"Well, what do you know? The best-looking couple in Bryson City is sharing breakfast with us," Sally told them as she walked up to the table.

"Hi, Sally," Susan said.

"How have you been doing, sweetheart?" asked Sally.

Susan smiled, "I'm doing very well. Thanks."

As the group placed their orders, Barry laid his hand on the journal, trying to hide it from anyone looking. "Okay, guys, it'll be ready soon," Sally said, walking towards the kitchen.

"What is that?" Doyle asked Barry, pointing at the journal.

Barry looked around, then leaned forward, "Ever since my stroke ten years ago, I have been having these dreams. I had dreams about burying this journal in my backyard. Your mom, Doyle, kept telling

me it was just a figment of my imagination. In those dreams, I would chase the devil I told you about through the mountains. It would always run behind our house and stand beside a small hole. I could read its thoughts because it never spoke. Instead, I understood I was to dig up the journal and learn the truth."

"What truth?" asked Doyle.

"Hang on, and I'll get to that. So, for the past six months, I've been getting up early, before your mom got up, and would dig holes in the backyard. I would save the top grassy section and place it back on top to keep your mom from noticing the spots. Two days ago, I finally found a box with this journal and several of my badges buried about eight inches deep."

Barry reached into his shirt pocket, removed a security badge, and laid it on the table. "What do you make of this?" he asked Doyle.

Doyle picked the badge up, put on his reading glasses, and looked it over. On the front of the badge was a picture of a young Barry Anderson with the words *top-secret clearance, Patriots Group*. "What the…" he said, looking up at Barry.

Barry nodded his head, staring at Doyle. "Everyone thought I was losing my mind, hell. Even I thought I was. I kept having these broken memories pop up in my head about that devil I always talked about with you guys. The weird thing is that I can remember all my cases as sheriff, several encounters with that devil, and the memories

with the family. But nothing about any of this work with the Patriots Group." he replied, grabbing the journal and opening it.

Sally and one of the cooks walked up to the table with their breakfast. "Here you go, guys. Enjoy."

"Thank you, Sal," Doyle replied, then turned to Barry. "So, you worked with the group I'm with now. That's crazy."

"Doyle, this journal has the date I started working with the Patriots Group and every case I worked on over the years."

"Do you think the stroke is why you forgot all this?" Doyle asked.

Barry shook his head, "No. I believe they erased my memory, and that caused the stroke. They removed my memories of the Patriots group and left everything else alone. I kept feeling that Deja Vu when we were under the Cracked-egg restaurant last year. When I started reading through this journal, I found out why. Under the Cracked-egg, that bunker was the headquarters for the division of the Patriots Group I was assigned. But, I used a different entrance than the one in the Cracked-egg. My notes only say that my office was at the marina, with a door to the bunker. I'm planning on going over there to look around soon. Maybe something there will trigger my memory."

Susan remained quiet while eating breakfast and listened to what the two guys said. Through the years, she learned only to add her thoughts if they asked her. Plus, she knew that the less she knew, the safer she'd be.

"Doyle, do you know where your next mission will be?" Barry asked.

Doyle wiped his mouth with a paper towel, "Yeah. In two weeks, they are sending me to the Crazy Mountains in Montana on a case. But, first, I have to stop by Edwards in California."

"Wonderful!" exclaimed Barry.

"Why is that, Dad?"

Barry looked around the diner again. "According to the journal, my fourth case was out in the Crazy Mountains. It had ties to here in the Smokies, but it was a case we didn't solve. What is your case about, Doyle?"

"From what I understand, my case has something to do with a female Indian medicine doctor. When I read over the report, five hikers have gone missing in the crazies in thirteen months. The locals believed that she, the medical doctor, played a role in their disappearances," Doyle told Barry.

"Yes, that is what I was involved in back in the 1980s. Every forty years, the legend is that this female Indian witch doctor appears and takes six people. But, of course, she's a witch, not a doctor, Doyle," explained Barry.

Doyle nodded in agreement and took a sip of coffee. "So, Dad, did you find any of the missing in the 80s?"

Barry opened the journal, "According to my notes, no. None of them. I wish I could remember this case for you, Doyle," he said before hitting his fist on the journal.

Susan reached up and placed her hand on Barry's. "It's okay. Don't try to force it, and maybe it'll come back to you."

"Thanks," Barry replied, then looked at Doyle, "The notes say that the locals would draw a picture of the witch on a tree, and where the heart would be, they would drive a nail in it. Then, every day, they would drive the nail in a little further, and by the time it was completely in, it would cause the witch to leave, even if she didn't have all of her victims."

"That is interesting. Dad, is there anything in your notes saying if you saw this witch?"

Barry flipped through the journal, "Dadgummit, there is a page missing at the end of this case. Now, why would I tear a page out?"

"That's not like you, dad. I've seen your notes on cases; they are very detailed indeed," Doyle said.

"Doyle, is this a case they think the Shadow Government is involved in?" Susan asked.

"No, it has nothing to do with the SG or even Miller if he is still alive. They are sending me there for two weeks to see what I can find out. They want me to research six locations where people have mysteriously gone missing. They are trying to keep me from the SG after what happened in California."

"You are going alone?" she asked.

"That is what they said. But, I was wondering if you felt up to it?" Doyle asked Susan.

"Absolutely!" she replied louder than she meant before putting her hand over her mouth.

Barry closed the journal, "Son, just be careful. Every missing person case has something to do with the Shadow Government."

"I'll keep that in mind, Dad. But, Susan, I want you to know that if it feels dangerous at any time, you must stay at the hotel," Doyle explained.

"Deal," replied Susan.

Doyle nodded, "Okay, We'll stop by Mike's house when we arrive in California. Susan, you can stay there while I travel to the Edwards facility".

"So, Dad, you said the witch had ties back in the Smokies. What did you mean by that?" asked Doyle.

Barry shook his head. "I'm not sure. One note I wrote mentioned that I saw a similar witch in the Smokies. Other than that, I'm not sure. I just hope my memory comes back soon. Anyway, next week, I'm flying to Maine to do some hunting with an old friend. Maybe that will help relax me."

"Exciting stuff. What about mom? Will she be okay by herself?" Doyle asked.

"Oh yeah, she'll be fine. Her sister is coming to spend a month at our home, so it'll be good for me to get out of the house," Barry said, laughing.

"Barry. That's not nice to say," Susan scolded him.

"Yeah, I know. But it's true," replied Barry.

"Sally, we're ready for the check," Doyle yelled.

"Sure thing, hun," Sally replied, walking over to their table and pulling the check from her apron. "Here you are, sweetie."

"Listen, Doyle. You need to talk to Harold before you head to Montana. He's an Indian, so he might have some information to help you. And, I believe he was or is part of the Patriots Group," explained Barry.

Doyle looked up from signing the receipt, "What makes you think that, Dad?"

"He was there below the restaurant with us, wasn't he? Do you think they would allow him in that room if he weren't?" asked Barry.

"That's true," Doyle replied, nodding his head.

Barry leaned closer, "Plus, I wrote his name several times in my journal."

"Well then, that proves it. You guys ready to go?" asked Doyle.

"I'm ready," replied Susan.

Doyle dropped a twenty-dollar bill on the table. As the trio exited the restaurant, Doyle and Susan turned toward their truck when Bar-

ry yelled, "Crap, I forgot to tell you guys. Friday, they are giving me an award in Washington for having served the country in law enforcement for all those years. I would like it if you guys could attend."

"Sure thing, Dad. We could use a little road trip," replied Doyle.

"Great! Your mom and I are flying up Thursday, then spending the weekend in Fredericksburg with your Aunt. As I said, we are bringing her back to stay the month."

"Yeah, that's right," said Doyle as he opened the truck door.

"We'll see you guys there," replied Susan.

"Okay. I'll text you all the information. Thanks, guys. I love you all," Barry told them, climbing into his truck.

"I love you too, Dad," Doyle yelled, then started the truck and drove away.

As the couple drove through Bryson City, Susan turned to Doyle, "We haven't been to DC in a long time. Together, anyway."

"DC is a swamp full of rats," Doyle replied, stopping at a traffic light.

"Yeah, I know. Maybe we'll bump into some old friends," responded Susan.

"Maybe," Doyle said, handing her a bag with scraps of food in it. "Will you feed that to Gunner?"

"I sure will. Here you go, Gunner, ready for your breakfast?" She asked Gunner, turning around with the bag in her hand.

The couple drove toward their home on Fontana Lake.

Barry pulled into Harold's driveway and blew the horn.

Jonah's owl, following orders, flies just out of sight, following Doyle's truck.

CHAPTER THREE

THE SWAMP AND THE RATS

"**A**gain, I would like to thank everyone I worked alongside during my thirty-plus years. Thank you all for this award," Barry said as he walked away from the podium.

Every table in the ballroom was full of current and former law enforcement officers and their families. This black-tie awards ceremony drew thousands of people and some of the best cooks in Washington, DC.

"Ladies and gentlemen, thank you for attending this afternoon. I hope that, for the ones who have to go back to work, you didn't overeat. Thank you, and we'll see all of you next year!" the host yelled to the crowd.

Doyle stands up and helps his mom to her feet, "Thanks, dear," she said.

"You are welcome," Doyle replied, then helped Susan up.

A bald gentleman walks up to Doyle, "Well, well. If it ain't Master Sergeant Anderson."

"Hey! Billy!" Doyle said as the two guys hugged, then Doyle turned to Susan. "Honey, this is Warrant Perkins or just Billy. He flew us off the mountain in California last year. He is the best mountain rescue helicopter operator in North America."

"I don't know about that," Billy said as he shook Susan's hand.

"I've heard many good things about you, Billy," she replied.

Doyle noticed that Billy had a cast on his leg from the knee down, "What did you do to your leg?"

Billy slapped Doyle on the back, "Oh, it's nothing. I took a little fall in the mountains. How's your leg after the surgery, Doyle? I also heard about you finding that young boy in the Smokies last year." He looked at Susan, "Your husband is the best, hands down."

Doyle nodded, "Thanks, but I haven't reached your level yet. My leg is good, thanks for asking."

"The word on the street is that you ran into something supernatural during that search. Is there any truth to that?" Billy asked.

Doyle laughed, putting his arm around him, "Billy, you can't believe everything you hear. You know that."

"Oh, I see. You understand, don't you, Susan? When Doyle doesn't answer with a definite no, the answer is always yes."

"You got me," Doyle said as Billy's cell phone chimed.

"Doyle, I've got to run, but I wanted to know if you'd be interested in teaching a few SAR classes for me this fall?"

"Sure, I would. Where?"

"Upstate New York is the location. Hey, I've got to go. I'll call you next month to set it up," Billy said as he limped off.

"Sure thing, Billy."

Barry returned to the table, holding his plaque for his time served on search and rescue missions as a cop. Doyle shook his hand, "Congrats, dad."

"Thanks, son. Oh shit, here comes Douglas. Come on, honey, let's get out of here before he sees us," he said to his wife, Stella. "I'll see you guys back at home Monday," Barry told them as he and Stella darted toward the exit.

"Doyle, it's excellent to see you again," Senator Douglas said, walking up to him and Susan.

Doyle looked up from the pamphlet, acting like he was reading, "Senator, I thought I smelled something rotting."

The Senator laughed and pointed at Doyle, "You're funny, just like your old man." The senator reached out his hand to Susan, "looking good as always,"

Susan shook his hand, "Thank you, Stanley."

"Are you two staying here in DC tonight?"

"No. We are not," Doyle snapped, reaching up and removing the Senator's hand from Susans.

"Oh now, come on, man. Are you still upset about that Benghazi thing?" the Senator asked Doyle.

"Senator, if you'll excuse us," Doyle said as he and Susan walked away.

"You are just as stubborn as your old man!" Yelled the Senator. "Miller was right about you!"

Doyle turned around, "Why, you fat son-of-a-..." he said before Susan jerked on his arm and guided him towards the exit.

"I'll be seeing you soon, Senator," Doyle shouted to him before he left the room.

"Is that a threat, Doyle?" the Senator asked.

"It's a guarantee!" snapped Doyle as he and Susan exited the ballroom.

The ballroom became quiet as the remaining people looked at the Senator. "It's okay, people. We are old friends, just teasing each other," the Senator said, motioning for everyone to go about their business. Then, an FBI agent approached the senator, "Sir, I have two agents following Barry Anderson and his wife waiting for the call to pick them up."

"Excellent. Go ahead and detain Barry. I'm flying up to my ranch in Wisconsin. Bring Barry to me there; I'll take care of him once and for all."

"Sir, what about Barry's wife? Should we detain her as well?" the agent asked.

The Senator reached down and picked up a half-full glass of Bourbon, "No. throw her in a ditch or kill her. I don't care," he replied before drinking.

"Yes, sir."

Oh, and get my plane ready. I've been waiting for this day for years," the Senator said as he laughed.

"Yes, sir," the FBI agent replied.

"Babe, don't make a scene over that no-good old fart," Susan told Doyle as they exited the hotel onto the sidewalk.

"I know, sorry. But, unfortunately, the piece of crap knows how to push my buttons."

"Of course he does. That's why he does it. He knows that it's a raw spot for you, and he loves to poke it," she told him while rubbing his back.

"And he knows he has protection in this city. I'll catch him out sometime…." Doyle started to say before stopping himself. "No, I don't mean that…if Big Brother is listening."

They laughed before Doyle asked, "You want to ride to Arlington National Cemetery?"

"Sure, that sounds good."

"We can't come to DC without stopping by and seeing Bullseye," he said to her, pulling out his phone and opening a shuttle app.

"I knew that. Plus, that place is so peaceful, just being around all those heroes," she said.

"Over there, babe," he told her, pointing to a small car that had just pulled over and its driver waving at them. The two walked over and climbed into the backseat of the small car. As they drove through DC, Doyle saw the Presidential helicopters fly overhead, making their way toward the White House.

"Why would anyone in their right mind want to be President?" he asked.

Susan smiled, "I think you answered your question, dear."

"Yeah. I guess I did, uh," Doyle said, laughing.

1543 HOURS
PRESENT-DAY
ARLINGTON NATIONAL CEMETERY

A slight breeze blew through the trees, and the smell of freshly cut grass filled the air. Rows of white headstones that go on as far as the eye can see stand bright in the afternoon sun. Dogwood and Redbud trees are in full bloom, with white and red colors that sway in the

breeze. Susan stood patiently waiting at the end of one row as Doyle kneeled facing his friend's grave marker, twenty yards away.

"I wish I could tell you things have gotten better, buddy. But they haven't. At least Miller finally got what he had coming," Susan heard him say as she watched him pat the grave marker. He then stood up and saluted it before turning to walk toward her. She noticed when he got closer that he had tears in his eyes.

"Oh, baby," she said, grabbing and hugging him.

"I'm okay, dear. Let's walk around for a while, maybe stop by JFK's gravesite. If you want to?" he asked.

"Sure," she responded.

As they entered the circular walkway to JFK's gravesite, an older gentleman walked past them. "Good afternoon, Sergeant Anderson," he said as he walked by.

"Good Afternoon," Doyle said as he stopped and looked at the man, "Do I know you, Sir?"

The gentleman stopped and turned to face them, "I'm sure you don't, or shouldn't. But I know you. Nice to meet you finally, Susan," he said, removing his gray fedora hat with a black band from his head.

"Nice to meet you, too," she replied hesitantly.

Doyle reached out and shook the gentleman's hand. Before he could ask again who he was, the old man cut him off, saying, "You served under my command back in 1990 in Iraq."

"Oh, okay. Your name slipped my mind, sorry."

"You wouldn't know my name, Doyle. I was the tenth five-star general in America's history," the gentleman explained.

Doyle chuckled, "There have only been nine five-star generals. So... if you'll excuse us," he said as they turned to walk away.

"Officially, that is," he said to Doyle before continuing. "You stopped by to see Bullseye, who, might I add, was shot down by Colonel Miller in Afghanistan. Colonel Miller met his demise in California a few months back when he tried to attack you and Mr. Prine, or Jonah, as he goes by now. But Miller phoned you at Fort Bragg after your surgery that I paid for to let you know he is still alive."

Doyle and Susan stopped walking and slowly turned back around. "How did you know that?" Doyle asked.

"I know everything about you, Doyle. Many years ago, I hired your dad to help me with my Patriot group fight to stop the Shadow Government's plan for a one-world system. Your mother also worked for me. You are one of the few within our group to ever lay eyes on me or even to know I exist."

"I doubt my mom had anything to do with you or your group. What's your name?" asked Doyle.

"Oh, but she did. My name is General X," he replied, walking towards them.

Susan grabbed Doyle's hand and slid behind him.

General X smiled, "Don't worry, Susan. Right now is the safest you have ever been in your entire life. Two soldiers in invisible suits, a few feet away from you, protect us. Also, one of my satellites monitors us roughly thirteen thousand miles above. The lens on it is so powerful that it can tell what color your shoelaces are," General X explained as he motioned for the soldiers to reveal themselves.

Doyle and Susan notice two soldiers slowly appearing on both sides of them before they disappear again. Susan grabbed Doyle's hand even tighter.

"What can I do for you, General X?" asked Doyle.

"Just call me General. Isn't it interesting that we finally meet at the place honoring one of the greatest Presidents in the history of the United States of America that the Shadow Government had killed?" asked the General.

Doyle looked around, "Yeah, I would say it is."

The General looked at Susan and said, "My lady, would you be so kind as to excuse us for maybe thirty minutes so Doyle and I could go for a walk and talk? I assure you that you and your husband have my word, and no harm will come to you."

Doyle turned to Susan. "It's okay, babe. You said you wanted some exercise, so here is your chance."

"If you would go in that direction, we'll go the other way. Then, when we meet back up, you two are free to go," the General explained to her.

"Okay," Susan responded before kissing Doyle and walking away.

"You have a nice-looking woman there, Doyle. My Betty died six years ago, and she was ninety-seven. She was a year older than me," explained the General.

"So, you are a hundred and two?" asked Doyle.

"That I am. I don't need a cane to walk, hearing aids to hear, or readers to read. Pretty impressive, uh?"

Doyle shook his head, "I'd say it's more than impressive...."

17 10 HOURS
PRESENT-DAY
VIRGINIA WELCOME CENTER, OFF I95

Barry pulled the car into a parking space near the restroom building. "Hang on, honey. If I don't stop, I will wet my pants."

"Okay. I'm going to walk around while you're gone. My feet are aching," Stella told him as he jogged towards the door, holding his crotch.

She walked up the sidewalk, which winded around through tall trees between the car and semi-truck parking areas. She stopped

beside a trash can to empty her pockets of candy wrappers when she noticed two SUVs pull up beside their vehicle. Four men jumped out, holding pistols, and ran into the building with both drivers seated behind the wheel for a quick escape. Stella knew this was not good, and being married to Barry for over fifty years, she knew she had to hide. He always told her it was better for her to survive than to try and save him if anyone ever came after them.

"My goodness, that sure feels better," Barry said out loud, walking out of the rest-stops bathroom. He turned to look at the state map hanging on the wall when he felt the familiar feeling of the cold steel touching the back of his neck.

"Don't move an inch, old man," Barry heard a man's voice say.

Barry slowly raised his hands, "Just go easy, son."

"I'm not your son, you scum bag."

"If I were a little younger, I'd make you eat those words, punk," replied Barry, slowly looking around to see how many guys were there.

"I hate to say it, old man, but we outnumber you. Hell, it would only take one of us," one of the other guys said as the four laughed.

Barry laughed while nodding, "Then why did the Senator send four of you if it would only take one to pick up an almost eighty-year-old?"

"Shut up. " Where is the wife?" the man holding the gun to Barry's head asked.

"She stayed in DC, lad."

The man returned his gun to its holster and turned Barry around, saying, "Don't lie to me, and don't call me lad." He reached up and grabbed Barry by the shirt collar.

Barry punched the man in the mid-section in a flash, then grabbed the man's arm and turned around, twisting the arm upside down. Next, Barry used his opposite arm and pushed his weight into the man's arm, dislocating his elbow. "Never put away your weapon, lad!" Barry snapped.

One of the other guys walked over and hit Barry in the head with his pistol, knocking Barry out cold. "Go outside and find the wife," he told the other two.

The man with the dislocated elbow stands up and pops it back into place, "Shit! That freaking hurt." He walked over and kicked Barry in the midsection.

"Help me drag Barry outside before we draw attention," the man who hit Barry said.

They picked him up, swinging both of Barry's arms over their shoulders, and started to walk him back to the SUVs. The other two guys split up, looking for Stella outside.

"Just relax. The guys can't see you in here," a truck driver said to Stella.

After the guys from the SUVs entered the reststop building, Stella ran out into the truck parking area. She noticed one older gentleman starting to climb back into his rig. "Sir, can I hide in your truck? Those men over there are chasing me."

"Excuse me?" the trucker asked.

"My husband is a retired federal agent, and these guys are trying to kill us."

"What guys, where are they?" he asked.

"The men who pulled up in those two black SUVs are in the building now, doing God knows what to my husband."

"We just can't sit here. We need to help!" snapped the trucker.

"No. You don't understand. Those guys are black-ops guys, military. They'll kill you and then me," explained Stella.

"Okay. Climb in the sleeper. My windows are tinted so that nobody can see in," the trucker told her, climbing into the big rig after she did. After he closed the door, he reached back into the sleeper and pulled out a sawed-off shotgun. "Here, ma'am, you hang on to this. I have a .45 handgun up here."

The trucker watched as the two men in black suits searched through the truck parking area. He looked back towards the restroom building and, through the trees, could barely make out two other guys dragging someone to one of the SUVs. He held tight on the grip of the Colt .45 as one of the men walked around his truck. Stella sat on her

knees off to the passenger side of the sleeper, holding the shotgun, praying that Barry would be okay.

Standing by the SUVs, one of the men whistled loudly, "Let's go, forget about her. We got the most important one." After he said that, he climbed into Barry's car, started it up, backed out, and drove off.

The two SUVs backed out of the parking spots as the other two guys ran over and climbed in, then both SUVs sped off and were out of sight in seconds.

"Ma'am, do I need to call someone for you?" asked the trucker.

"No. I'm sure those guys are monitoring all the calls in this area. Is there any chance you are heading south?"

"Yes, ma'am, I am."

"Would you mind dropping me off at the next exit, down by the high school? My sister lives there."

"Yes, ma'am. That's the least I could do for you. Do you have a phone?"

Stella shook her head. "No. Everything I had was in the car. We better get going. They'll soon find out that my sister lives nearby and will arrive at her house.

The trucker started the semi and pulled out of the parking space. Stella leaned forward, "Do you have a pencil and some paper?"

"Yes, ma'am. A few pockets on the back wall have plenty of both."

"Okay. I'm going to write down a number for you. Call this number once you get down the road fifty miles. When the man answers, I want you to say that the cell is separated. Then, hang up. It's a secured number, and your number will not be used or stored."

"Okay. What does that mean?" the trucker asked Stella.

"It is a code for the group we work for that means one of us is in trouble," she replied, looking at several business cards in the pocket. "Is this your name and current address on this card?"

The trucker looked at her, "Oh shit. Yes, that is my name and address."

"It's okay, honey. I will not share it. Instead, I will send you money for your troubles and for helping me."

"Thank you, ma'am. But that's not necessary."

They pulled off the interstate at the exit. Stella had asked him to "Stay to the right, and then the high school will be on your right."

"Yes, ma'am."

"Once you turn onto the road that leads to the high school, drive just past it and stay to the right by the football stadium," she explained as the trucker turned by the school.

"I see the football stadium," he said.

"Okay. Just past the stadium, you will see a parking lot on the right by the practice fields. Pull in there, and I can walk to my sisters."

The trucker followed her directions to a tee and stopped the semi in the parking lot. The air brakes hissed as the air was released from the system. "Here you are, ma'am."

"Thank you so much. Where should I lay this shotgun?" Stella asked, holding it up for him to see.

"Just on the bed, there is fine," he replied, then climbed out of the rig to help her down.

"Are you a secret agent, ma'am?"

"No, sir. Both my husband and I have been fighting government corruption for years. The bad guys won't go down without a fight. Again, thank you so much. Now, you need to get going. You never saw me, okay?"

"Yes. ma'am."

"Remember. At fifty miles, make that call," Stella yelled back to him as she jogged into the woods beside the practice field.

The trucker removed his hat, rubbed his head, and waved to her, "I will!" He turned to climb back into the truck, then turned around, watching her disappear into the trees, "Nice butt for an older lady."

Stella hid in the wooded area until the truck drove out of sight. She then jogged across the road and up her sister's driveway. After walking to the back of the house, she climbed over the fence. Then, seeing her sister standing at the kitchen sink through the glass door, she tapped on the glass.

"Oh my goodness, Stella. You startled me."

"Rose, we are in trouble," Stella said as Rose opened the door.

"What kind of trouble? Where's Barry?" she asked.

Stella walked in and turned around to close the curtains over the sliding doors, "We are not safe here. We have to leave."

"What in heaven's name are you talking about, Stella?"

"I'll explain everything once we get out of here."

"Where are we going? I have my bags packed to stay at your house. I need to load them in the car," explained Rose.

"We don't have time for that. We are not going to my house. They will be looking for me there. We have to get to the safe house outside of Manassas."

Rose stared at her briefly, "I don't understand."

"The Shadow Government has kidnaped Barry, and they will be looking for us soon. I have asked the trucker who dropped me off to message Barry's partner, Harold. He will send protection for us, but we have to get to a safe location," Stella explained.

"I always told you the work that Barry was doing would get you in trouble one day!" snapped Rose.

"I don't have time to debate with you. Get your ass moving, and let's get out of here. If you want to live," Stella responded, walking over and opening the door to the garage.

Rose jerked her purse off the bar. Then, as she walked past Stella, she mumbled, "Talk to me like that in my house, will you."

"I'm sorry, Rose. But you don't know the type of people we are dealing with," Stella said as she moved around to get in the car.

"So, I guess this means I won't be staying at your house for the next month?" Rose asked.

Stella closed the passenger's door and unplugged Rose's phone from the charger. "No phones or any electronic devices," Stella explained.

Rose started the car and opened the garage door. "Are you and Barry mixed up in drugs or something?" Rose asked.

"Of course not. Don't be silly. We both worked for the government with the Patriot's Group. Our involvement with the group was top secret. But, since we may not live to see the morning, I can finally tell you."

Rose pulled out of the garage, "What's the Patriot's Group?"

"Turn left, Rose. We are going to take the back roads. This is a group that fights corruption around the world, but mostly here in the United States."

Rose sat quietly for a moment, "What did you do?"

Stella looked at her sister, "Barry was a tracker, and I was a sniper."

Rose slammed on the brakes, "A snipper? You mean you killed people?"

"Well, that's what a sniper does. Yes, several, but only terrorists. Keep driving! We have to stay focused on the task at hand. And that is getting to the safe house."

Rose released the brake and pressed the gas pedal, "I cannot believe my sister is a killer. Dear Lord, what is the world coming to?" she asked, looking up.

"I'm not a killer. I'm a Patriot. Huge difference, Rose."

"Did you kill people? Then that makes you a killer. What will you kill me if I don't drive fast enough? Uh? Are you?" Rose asked, her voice shaking. "My God. You are a grandmother!"

"Just drive and be quiet. I'll explain more to you later," Stella told her.

Rose looked at her, then back to the road, "My older sister is Jannie Bond."

Rose and Stella continued driving to the safe house.

Doyle and General X prepared to start their conversation.

Barry started to wake in a small aircraft hangar outside of Washington, D.C.

CHAPTER FOUR
GENERAL X
★★★★★

1800 HOURS
PRESENT-DAY
ARLINGTON NATIONAL CEMETERY

"I want to thank you for joining me for this walk and chat, Sergeant Anderson," General **X** said to him.

Doyle nodded in agreement as the two men walked away from JFK's gravesite. "Not a problem, General. Please call me Doyle."

"Very well, Doyle. The only way I know how to explain this to you is to start from the beginning. I was born in 1919 in a rural little town in Virginia. My father was Irish, and my mother was Jewish. My mother's lineage goes back to Joseph of Arimathea. You know, the man responsible for the burial of Christ?" the General asked.

"Yes, I know who he is," responded Doyle.

"I figured you did. Anyhow, my father's lineage was never fully known or, to better say it, understood. My earliest memory of him

was of us traveling to Jerusalem in 1921 at two and a half years old. Most people say there is no way I can remember something at that age, but I most certainly do, I tell you. Father had taken me out into the desert, east of the city, towards Jericho, where we were to camp for three days. We met up with four of my father's Jewish friends, who were part of the Haganah, the main paramilitary of the Jewish population of that time."

Doyle looked at the General. "I know who they were. They served from 1920 until 1948 when Israel became a nation, and then they became part of the Unified Armed Forces or the Israel Defense Forces."

The General tipped his hat to a lady walking past them, then turned to Doyle. "Excellent, Doyle. Your knowledge is impressive, most impressive. So, I was too young to know or understand why my father was camping with these gentlemen. Looking back, I assume it had something to do with the coming war. We set up camp just west of the Jordan River in an open plain where you could see the open desert for miles. Father stayed up chatting with his friends after he put me to bed in one of the larger tents with two other children. It was chilly, and I had no problem falling asleep once tucked into my sleeping bag. I was awakened several hours later by a bright light shining through a small opening in the tent. I sat up and noticed my father was sleeping beside me, and everyone was fast asleep. So I climbed out of my sleeping bag and walked outside, and that's when I saw it."

The two men came to a bench along the path through the cemetery, "Doyle, let us have a seat for a spell."

"Sounds good, General," Doyle responded.

A small group of ROTC cadets walked past them, "Oh, the joy of being young," General **X** said to Doyle.

1835 HOURS
PRESENT-DAY
NOKESVILLE, VIRGINIA.

"Stella, I'm stopping here. We need gas for the car." Rose explained to her.

Stella looked around the small gas station parking lot, "Okay. Pull up to that outside pump. I'm staying put because I don't want anyone to see me. They are always watching. They have access to all security cameras nationwide."

Rose pulled up beside the gas pump and put the car in park. As she turned off the ignition, she turned to Stella, "Before I get out of this car, you are going to explain to me what's happening. No more half-truths or bullshit."

"Rose. We don't have time for this. We're just a few miles from the safe house."

"I don't care! I want some answers, now!" snapped Rose.

Stella exhaled before she started, "Barry and I were recruited in the 1960s, not long after the assassination of JFK, to help fight government corruption. Barry worked on cases of missing people, and I mainly worked on security details for a high-ranking general. I was a

long-range sniper. Remember all those shooting contests Dad entered me in when we were kids?

"I remember all the ones you won," Rose replied, rolling her eyes.

"Well, that caught the eye of some influential people in Virginia. I was the daughter of a secret service man and, later, a sheriff's wife. Plus, I was one of the best shooters in the country," Stella told her.

"I always knew you and Dad were up to more than just skeet shooting," Rose replied, shaking her head.

"Dad was the reason I joined the Patriots group. He was also a high-ranking official. Barry didn't know for some time that I was part of the group. Dad helped recruit him for his searching skills, but Barry could never know my role. The Shadow government would use it against him if they knew," Stella said, looking around to see if anyone was watching.

"For five years, I worked overseas mostly, protecting the General. He is one of the founding members of the Patriots Group. He was close to JFK, and those that killed JFK wanted him dead as well," explained Stella to Rose.

"I never would have thought a group like that ever existed. Plus, Barry wasn't a military man. So why would they use him?" asked Rose.

"As I said, Rose. It was for his searching abilities, nothing more."

"And Doyle?" Rose asked, looking directly at Stella.

"He is in the group now as well. That was Dad's idea before he died. Dad chose the gentleman we're meeting at the safe house to recruit Doyle as well," responded Stella.

Rose put her hand over her mouth and asked, "What about your two sons? Will they also join the group?"

"No. Dad and Barry agreed with the Patriots group that they were not to be brought into this ever!" snapped Stella.

"What agreement did they make?" Rose asked hesitantly.

Stella turned to Rose, "That dad would not seek treatment for his cancer, and Barry would have his memory wiped."

"My goodness. You were working for the devil!" Rose snapped.

"Rose, I'm sure you don't know about the devil. I could show you pictures of what the devil can do if you'd like. Now, we need to fuel this car and get moving."

"I bet you could," Stella mumbled as she climbed out of the car.

"Don't run your mouth. Just fuel the car, sis," Stella said as she pointed, with her thumb, toward the car's rear.

Rose hissed, then walked up to the gas pump.

1840 HOURS
PRESENT-DAY
ARLINGTON NATIONAL CEMETARY

"As I was saying, Doyle," the General said before continuing. "That's when I saw a large bronze disc floating in the sky. I could

see people inside looking out of windows as this disc hovered there. Then, off to the right of it, I saw six men standing there. One held an inkhorn and wrote things on a piece of papyrus. I stood there frozen in fear; I couldn't move even if I wanted to. Finally, the man holding the inkhorn looked at me, raising the paper. That's when I heard his voice say, You have been marked upon your forehead to fulfill a mission. You will seek out and destroy those who work in abominations against those with the same mark as you."

Doyle sat there hanging on every word the general spoke. "What happened next, Sir?"

"He showed me future events, wars, and things I was too young to understand. But what he showed me that night was burned into my memory for life. I woke the following day back inside the tent. I did not speak of it with my father because I felt I wasn't allowed to tell anyone. But, from that day forward, I could see the people who had the mark and those who did not," the General told him.

"What does the mark look like, Sir?"

The General turned to face Doyle, "It is very faint and almost looks like a smear," he said, pointing to Doyle's forehead.

Doyle reached up and rubbed his forehead, "I have the mark?"

"Indeed you do, Doyle. Yours, however, is different. It looks like the star of David."

"What does that mean, Sir?"

The General laughed, "I have no idea. But, it must mean somebody specifically chose you."

The two men sat there for several minutes without saying a word as a group of people walked past them. "Not one of those people has the mark," the General said, then turned to Doyle.

"Now, that does not mean they are bad people. This part took me about thirty years to figure out. But first, I had to learn how to discern those who are not knowledgeable about the world's truth and those who are evil. Not having the mark doesn't make you evil."

The General put his arm on the back of the bench, around Doyle, "People have been taught for generations that we exist within an objective universe, but science and data show that we live in a manufactured and interactive matrix. But, unfortunately, corporate and military interests have hijacked science research."

"That's interesting. I have felt our government has used science to hide the truth for years," Doyle told him.

"Exactly. What is one of the enormous lies of today, Doyle? Climate change. The proof is that the sun is the most significant factor regarding climate change, not carbon dioxide. The ice is not melting the way they want us to believe. It is all a form of fear and control. You control the masses, and you control the power."

Doyle nodded his head, "I agree, General."

"I know you've heard this before, Doyle. But, the greatest deception the devil has ever pulled off is convincing people that he doesn't exist," replied the General.

The General looked around and then up to the sky, "They also try to tell us that consciousness is the result of brain activity, which is invalid. Consciousness exists separately from the brain."

He turned to face Doyle, "We each have a soul. The world they have created has a clay foundation with a steel structure standing on top. It is top-heavy, and we are going to push it over."

"People have been trying that for centuries, Sir. So what makes us any different where we can succeed?" asked Doyle.

The General smiled, "Timing. The time has come."

"Again, people have thought the time was here before. I'll ask you again. Why is it now different?" Doyle asked, turning to face the General.

"Patience, Doyle. You will understand when the time is right. Just because it has begun doesn't mean it is tomorrow," the General said, patting Doyles back, then stood up.

1700 HOURS
PRESENT-DAY
SAFE HOUSE OUTSIDE MANASSAS, VIRGINIA

Stella directed Rose toward a small lane between a golf course and a junkyard. "After you cross the railroad tracks, take the second right and pull up to the gate," Stella told her.

"This place looks shady, Stella. I don't like it one bit!" snapped Rose.

Stella pointed at the turn ahead. "You'll be fine, I promise," she said, lowering the passenger-side window.

A guard approached the lowered window, "Ma'am, what is the passcode?"

"Megiddo-777," Stella responded.

The guard motioned to the guard shack to let them proceed, "Mrs. Anderson, they are expecting you."

"Thank you, Sergeant," she replied as Rose pulled through the gate.

Two more guards appeared and directed Rose into a parking place beside a small aircraft hangar. The two men assisted the women from the car. "Stella! Thank God you are okay," a gentleman said, exiting the hangar.

"Harold, so nice of you to join us," she replied.

"That truck driver relayed your message to me, and I went directly to the airport and flew here."

"They took Barry!" Stella snapped.

"Yes, I know. A few minutes ago, we intercepted a transmission that said they were taking Barry to meet with Senator Douglas. We know

the Senator is flying to Wisconsin, where he's spending a few weeks at his ranch. So we can only assume that is where they are taking Barry."

"Where at in Wisconsin?" asked Stella.

"Near Devils Lake, outside Baraboo," Harold replied, walking over to a wall map. "The Senator's property is in this location. We understand there are underground tunnels all through the area," he said, pointing at the map.

"That makes it easier for them to traffic children. Rats love their tunnels!" Stella snapped.

"I believe they will take Barry into those tunnels to make it harder for us to track him," replied Harold.

They stood there looking at the map before Stella turned to Harold. "Can you get me there?"

Harold looked at her, "I can, but you won't have any backup. All the teams are out of the country except for Team Papa, and they are in the crazy mountains preparing for Doyle's arrival."

"Harold, you damn well know I don't need any backup!" Stella growled, looking directly into his eyes.

"Now, Stella. You need to relax."

"Do not tell me to relax, Harold! I told you six years ago that Senator Douglas was getting too powerful and needed to be removed from his position."

"Keep your voice down. I understand what you are saying, but it wasn't easy then. Things today are different," Harold explained.

"You are damn right things have changed. I'm going to Wisconsin to rescue My husband and deal with the Senator myself!" snapped Stella.

Harold walked away from the map, "I understand. However, I believe that the Senator is setting a trap for Doyle. He knows that when Doyle finds out, he will rush there to save Barry."

"That will surely happen," Stella said as she followed behind Harold.

The two entered the hangar as another gentleman walked over to Rose. "Mrs., I will need you to follow me," he said as he directed her in the other direction.

"Yes. Okay," replied Rose.

"I think I have a good plan, Stella," Harold told her as he opened the door to a small office.

"And that would be what?" she replied as she noticed Leon standing in the office.

"Hello Stella," said Leon

She smiled and replied, "Hello, Leon."

"We will get you in the forest up in Wisconsin, armed with your choice of sniper rifles. I will ensure there is no radio chatter that Doyle could intercept. We will keep Doyle as busy as possible once he

lands in California. I spoke with Mike just before you arrived; he will stay with Doyle the entire time. Just like last year, per our request," Leon explained, sitting behind a desk. "That'll be all, Harold."

"Yes, sir," Harold replied, winking at Stella before closing the office door as he exited.

Stella walked over and leaned on the desk. "Leon, you are a good-hearted man who looks after his men. But, this mission will be bloody. The Senator has to go. The time for debating with him and hoping he will do the right thing is over."

Leon leaned back in the chair, "Stella, I understand. Even his group has that in mind because he has aligned himself with several liberal terrorist groups. Not to mention how Colonel Miller could access top-secret equipment and then steal that equipment. But the Patriots group cannot be a part of this. So you go in alone, and if something goes wrong, we will say you went rogue."

Stella nodded her head, "I understand, Leon."

"As soon as you arrive in Wisconsin, the entire state will go black. All forms of communication will go down. I have men working on that now. It will appear like an electrical failure," explained Leon.

"That'll work," replied Stella.

Leon leaned forward and placed his elbows on the desk. He put his right hand under his chin, "You will have no communication abilities with anyone outside that area. And you will only have ninety minutes to pull this off."

Stella laughed, "That's more than enough time."

"We will drop you off near the cliffs overlooking his ranch. Once you take the kill shot, you must exit quickly to safety. I'm still working on the details," Leon told her as he watched her facial expressions closely.

"That's the way I like it," she responded.

"I will send one of Jonah's owls there to help you," Leon replied, leaning back in the chair.

"Okay, I want Harold to go with me. Plus, I want my trusty M21 sniper rifle," replied Stella, smiling.

"Consider it done. As far as the Shadow Government knows, Harold is retired. If, and I emphasize the if, you eliminate the Senator, you'll have two to four other men to deal with afterward. I'll have your rifle and everything ready for you within the hour," Leon said, grabbing the phone.

"It'll be a walk in the park," she said.

Leon shook his head as he dialed a number on the phone, "If everything was as easy as it sounded. Yes, get me, Jonah, on the phone, please."

"Oh, it will be just that easy," Stella whispered as she sat in one of the office chairs.

17 15 HOURS
PRESENT-DAY
ARLINGTON NATIONAL CEMETERY

"How is the leg, Doyle?" the General asked.

"It's a whole lot better. Almost one hundred percent, I'd say," replied Doyle, rubbing his repaired leg.

"That's good. Let's walk some more. I understand Perkins stopped by to chat with you after the ceremony today?"

"Yes. That's correct, General."

"I instructed my men to break his leg for not protecting you during the California mission," the General replied.

Doyle turned to the General, "What?"

"He was in charge of the security for you, Mike, and Jonah. Unfortunately, you were injured, so he had to endure the same injury you suffered. An eye for an eye, Doyle. Things just run smoother when people are held accountable for their mistakes. Don't you think so, Doyle?" asked the General.

"With all due respect, Sir. But, no, I disagree with that. My injury was due to my action, not Perkins's mistake. I believe people should be held accountable for their actions, not the actions of others, Sir. Besides, he is a helicopter pilot and a damn good one. So what did he have to do with what was happening on the ground?"

"He is more than just a pilot. He is one of our controllers. But it is interesting, considering that I'm one of the most influential people

globally, and you are not afraid to stick to your beliefs even if that may cause tension between you and me," the General said before he turned and smiled at Doyle.

"I'm not trying to cause tension. I just believe in treating people right," Doyle replied, pulling a cigar from his pocket. "Plus, I paid the price with my blood not to have to kiss anyone's ass. Mind if I smoke?"

The General chuckled, "No, go right ahead."

Doyle lights the cigar and, as he's puffing on it, asks, "So, is Colonel Miller dead?"

Again, the General laughed, "You like to be in control of the conversation, don't you?"

Doyle shook his head, "No, not really. I just wanted to know if he survived the firefight, that's all."

"The Colonel. He is indeed alive," replied the General. "Did you think the attack force killed him, Doyle?"

Doyle took a long draw on the cigar, blowing the smoke out before answering. "No. I thought as much." He took another drag off the cigar, "One thing I will say about Miller, he is one tough S.O.B," he replied, blowing out the smoke and then turning toward the General. "Don't you think, sir?"

"There is a fine line between crazy and tough. But, yes, he is a strong individual. He survived that attack, but he is no longer in the dimension we are in." replied the General.

The two walked silently for several minutes before the General asked, "Have you ever heard of Memorandum 273?"

Doyle looked confused, "Yes, sir. It's the memorandum that essentially sent us to war in Vietnam."

"Yes, indeed it was. It completely reversed JFK's wishes for military actions in Vietnam. Yet, LBJ signed it the very day after JFK's assassination," explained the General.

"I understand there are a lot of controversies with some of that," Doyle replied.

The General turned to Doyle, "No controversy at all. I worked with JFK to keep us from entering that war in Vietnam. We were pulling everyone out by the end of 1965. But, you know, Doyle, after they killed him, I had to go into hiding for five years because JFK had directed me to be the point man on tearing the CIA apart. So even today, I must have protection from the threats of the Shadow Government."

"I have always been told that if you ever cross them, you are an enemy for life," Doyle responded.

"That's true, my friend. The only thing worse is to be our enemy," the General said before laughing. "Because that is what they are. They have never had America's best interest in mind. Only theirs and their

minions. It is finally coming to light that the FBI is just as corrupt as the CIA."

The General continued, "In the college state shooting in May 1970, the FBI fired the first shots. They are and have always been agitators."

"You mean their upper management, right? I know some very good people who worked for the Bureau their whole career, who are first-class people," replied Doyle.

The General laughed, "Of course there are. But I'd be willing to bet they knew something wasn't right. Won't many of them say the treatment of '45 was right?"

"No, that was as corrupt as it gets," Doyle agreed.

"Doyle, I could go on for hours about events like the Gulf of Tonkin that got us in the Vietnam War, all the anomalies that happened on 9/11, and even some lies about World War Two. But I feel I have taken up enough of your time. So, I do thank you for talking with me," said the General as he stopped walking.

Doyle stopped and turned to face him, "Sir. It was my pleasure."

The General reached into his pocket and handed Doyle a small gold coin. "I got this in Egpyt back in 1929. It's yours now."

Doyle took the coin and looked it over, "Sir, thank you."

"You keep this on you anytime you are out on a mission. I feel it is a good luck charm," replied the General.

Doyle looked up at him, "Thank you, Sir."

"Oh, look at the pretty red cardinal sitting on that grave marker," the General said, pointing at the bird.

Doyle turned to look at the bird, "Yes, I see it." He turned back to face the General, "What the, where did you go?" Doyle said, looking in all directions.

Doyle stood there looking around, holding the coin.

Stella reunites with her beloved sniper rifle in Manassas.

A small plane touched down in Wisconsin.

INTERLUDE
STELLA

There she is, my beautiful rifle. As the sergeant handed it to me, I felt a surge of gratitude. This rifle, my constant companion, has seen me through the darkest times, and its presence fills me with a sense of security and comfort. After what seemed like an eternity, Leon ended his conversation with Jonah.

"You look like you've met the love of your life," he said, smiling at me.

I turned and looked at him, then laid the rifle on the desk between us, "You could say that, Leon."

"She sure is a pretty weapon. You have taken good care of it through the years, Stella," he said, rubbing his hands on the rifle's stock. He looked like he was the one who was in love with my rifle. In reality, though, Leon hasn't fired a weapon since his injury while on deployment in Afghanistan.

"I sure would love to shoot it someday, if you don't mind, of course," he said with a boyish grin.

"Sorry, Leon. I'm retiring this weapon after this mission, and the Senator is dead," I told him, knowing it would annoy him. I enjoy pushing people's buttons. I picked it up from my dad; he was a champion at doing that. He was also a war veteran, and his influence on me is undeniable. I've always admired his strength and resilience, which I've strived to emulate. But also his detachment from the consequences of his actions, a trait I've inherited, for better or worse.

Leon frowned at me, "Oh, that's too bad. But that rifle has an extensive history, to say the least. It's been with you through thick and thin, hasn't it?"

"It has indeed. But, when I think about how many lives it has ended, I do not think I should keep it as a trophy," I explained, my voice tinged with a hint of regret and conflict. I'm torn between the rifle's role in my survival and the lives it has taken, a conflict that I'm not sure Leon or anyone can fully understand. Men are different about this kind of thing; they hold to items just like they like to stuff animal heads and nail them to the wall in their dens.

"Jonah is working on the details for this mission as we speak. He said he'd inform the leaders of the Patriot's group and then get back to me," Leon explained.

I have worked for the Patriots group longer than most members today have been alive, but Leon is good at what he does, and my son thinks a lot of him. However, I do not know this Jonah person.

"Okay. Thanks, Leon."

CHAPTER FIVE
UNDERGROUND RAILROAD

1800 HOURS
PRESENT-DAY
SAFE HOUSE, MANASSAS, VIRGINIA

"It's a go, Harold," Stella said to him as she walked out of the office.

Harold stood and walked alongside her as they headed into the small hangar. "That is what you wanted, correct?" he asked.

"Absolutely!" she snapped, then walked over to a soldier standing nearby. "Excuse me, do you know where they took my sister?"

The soldier turned to her, "Yes, Ma'am. We moved her to another location, where my men will keep her safe until this blows over."

"Very good. Sergeant," she replied.

Leon opened the office door and shouted to Harold, "Do you have a minute?"

"Yes, Sir," Harold replied as he turned and walked toward the office.

"Stella, give us just a minute," Leon told her as he closed the office door.

"Listen, Harold. There is no way I'm letting you and Stella go at this alone. She is one of the best shooters on the planet, but she is almost eighty. I just spoke with Jonah, and he will reroute Doyle to Wisconsin as soon as he lands in California," explained Leon.

"I understand. Why not send Doyle in from here?" Harold asked.

Leon shook his head, "We can't. The Shadow Government has to believe he is heading for the Crazy Mountains, or they'll warn the Senator that Doyle is heading to Wisconsin."

"I see," replied Harold.

"I feel the Senator kidnapped Barry on his own accord, and I don't believe the Shadow Government ordered it. He has always wanted to repay Barry for ruining his law enforcement career. So, that means the Senator will not have any special protection other than his security detail. I'll set you and Stella up in Wisconsin and then send Doyle to finish it. Does that sound good to you, Harold?"

"Yes. Thinking about it now, I would feel better with Doyle helping us out," Harold said, walking over and looking out of the office window at Stella, pacing back and forth, talking to herself.

"One condition. Stella does not know that Doyle is coming. She has to think it's just you two because I want her mind sharp. The Senator will not hesitate to kill her as well as Barry."

Harold stood for several seconds before he turned and responded, "Do not underestimate us because of our age. The Senator will never know we are there. But, you must remember, Indians do not age like the white man or, in your case, as the black man does. I still move around as if I'm in my forties."

"Harold, I meant no disrespect. I meant that you two should spend time with the grandchildren and not still work missions for the Patriot's Group," Leon replied.

"Great-grandchildren," responded Harold.

Leon walked to the office door. "As soon as Doyle arrives, you get Stella back to the train," he explained as he opened the door.

"Train?" asked Harold.

"That's correct. Jonah's train is hauling you two up to Wisconsin. Then, it's taking you and Barry back to North Carolina. The good thing about using his train is that it can run underground most of the way," Leon said as he motioned for Harold to exit the office with him.

"Yes, that's a good idea," said Harold, walking out of the office.

Leon walked over to Stella and said, "You and Harold are taking one of our trains to Wisconsin. A high-speed underground train should get you there in just four hours."

"Okay. Wow, that is interesting," responded Stella.

"Once you reach Wisconsin, I want both of you to remain on the train until 0400 hours. Then, one of my men will meet you to hand

over whatever gear you need. Enjoy the scenery. That is one of our biggest train depots in the midwest." Leon told her as they walked to the hangar's exit.

"It's already here?" asked Stella as she saw the train sitting on the tracks when Leon opened the door.

"Yes. You are the only passengers. Honestly, you are the only people on board. This train is fully automatic with its controllers in California," Harold said.

One of the train doors slid open as Stella and Harold walked over to it. A small set of steps lowered to the ground, and a handrail slowly folded against the steps.

"Wow! This is high-tech stuff," exclaimed Stella.

Harold walked to the side of the steps, "After you, my lady."

"Well, thank you, Harold," Stella told him as she climbed onto the train.

"I hope you two have a safe trip, and keep me posted on your progress," Leon told them, waving before turning and walking back into the hangar.

"Welcome aboard," a voice came over the intercom system on the train.

"Thank you," Stella replied.

"If you would please, cabin number four has been assigned to you for the trip to Wisconsin. It is the second door on the right," the voice said.

Stella and Harold walked down the hallway and entered the second door on the right. Cabin number four has one large main room with a conference table and chairs. It also has two separate bedrooms, each with a separate bathroom.

After Harold entered the cabin, the door closed and locked behind him. "What is going on here?" Harold asked, turning and pushing on the door.

The monitor on the front wall lights up, and Jonah appears on it. "Relax, Harold. It's locked for your safety. Everything you need is in this cabin."

"You know I do not like when I'm locked in," Harold responded to Jonah.

"I know, but trust me. Have I ever let you down?" Jonah asked.

Harold crossed his arms, "No, you have not."

Stella walked closer to the monitor, "Who are you?"

"Hello, Stella. I am Corey Prine, but I go by the name Jonah now. I am the leader of the North American division of the Patriots Group. I have worked with Harold for years and worked with your son, Doyle, last year."

"Nice to meet you," she replied.

"I'm also the head scientist with the Patriots Group and one of its founding members. This train you are aboard is one of my finest inventions, a high-speed underground stealth train."

"Underground? I didn't know we had underground trains," stated Stella.

"Oh, yes. We have over two thousand miles of track underground in just North America. We even have a tunnel beneath the Chukchi Sea into Russia that connects us with tracks worldwide beneath it," Jonah replied as the train started moving.

Stella sits on the couch and notices the desert passing by outside the window, "That is very interesting, Jonah. So tell me, why do I see desert in Virginia out of the window?"

"Those are not windows but a computer generation," Jonah said as he looked down. "Here, is that better?" he asked.

Stella now sees what she knows to be the countryside in Virginia, "Yes. That looks normal."

"I was wondering if you would notice that?" Jonah asked before continuing. "You see, most people that ride on this train do not know it goes underground, so we generate whatever scenery we need to keep them in the dark."

"I notice things that are not noticeable to the normal eye. Just like that ring you are wearing. Is that an ancient Egyptian lapis lazuli precious stone?" she asked Jonah.

"Very impressive, I must say. Yes, it is. We unearthed this ring many years ago on a dig I was part of in Egypt. This stone was a favorite of the ancient Egyptians for thousands of years. They believed it led the soul into immortality. Many also believed this royal stone contained the souls of the gods," explained Jonah.

"What do you believe?" Stella asked.

Jonah laughed, "You are outstanding. I see where Doyle gets it. It is just a neat ring. That's all I believe," replied Jonah, looking at the ring.

"Right.... So, what are our travel plans?" she asked, leaning back on the couch.

"In about ten minutes, we will enter the underground rail system, where we will stay until we get into Wisconsin. Then, the train will resurface near Lodi, Wisconsin, using the local tracks to the Devil's Lake area. Finally, you and Harold will exit the train below a bluff overlooking the Senators' ranch," Jonah replied.

"Where are our supplies and weapons?" asked Harold.

"That's right, here they are." After Jonah said that, the wall on both sides of the monitor slid open, revealing Stella's sniper rifle and all their gear.

"Nice," replied Stella.

Jonah smiled, "Everything you asked for is there, plus some gear I added to help with notifications if a soldier in an invisible suit gets near you."

"Invisible suit?" Stella asked.

"Ah yes, I have a video for you to watch, Stella. It will give you the information you'll need to know regarding the suits," Jonah said to her.

"That part is outside her purview," explained Harold.

"Yes, I know. But Stella needs to understand what to look for just to be safe. The Senator has a system installed around his ranch that keeps anyone in a suit from coming near it. But there will be about a mile from the tracks to the bluff where you won't be protected," Jonah told them.

"That's good to know," responded Harold, looking at Stella.

There is a small red box with two necklaces. Both of you are to wear one for the entire mission. It will beep if a soldier in an invisible suit gets within a hundred yards of you.

"So what you are saying is that we'll have seventeen hundred and sixty yards of no protection for an invisible suit attack?" asked Stella.

Jonah nodded his head, "That is what I am saying."

"This keeps getting more fun by the minute!" exclaimed Stella.

"Yep. I see where Doyle gets it," Jonah replied, laughing. "I would suggest that both of you get some rest. You will be there in four hours," Jonah said, looking at his watch.

"What about any camo clothing?" Stella asked.

They are in your bedrooms. Harold, your room is on the left. Stella, Your room is across from his. I will start the short video about suits on the TV in your room. Harold, I also have a video for you to watch about the Senator's security system and how to enter the ranch without being noticed.

"Sounds good," Harold replied.

"I'm going to power down the cabin except for your bedrooms so the train can go stealth. You both will not be allowed to leave the bedroom until we have resurfaced," Jonah told them.

"Great. Now I'm doubled locked in," snapped Harold.

Jonah smiled, "Harold, there are some pills on your nightstand to help you relax."

"You big baby," Stella replied, laughing as she entered her bedroom and closed the door.

"I don't like it when I'm locked in," Harold mumbled as he entered his bedroom and closed the door. Both doors locked with a loud crack, and the lights in the main room turned off. The train bounced and shook as it lowered itself into the underground tunnel. The TVs in both rooms lit up, and their videos began playing.

"Where in the world have you been, Doyle?" Susan asked as she approached him, sitting on a bench and staring at his phone.

"I have been right here the entire time," he replied.

"No, you haven't. "I walked past here twice, and you were nowhere to be seen," snapped Susan.

"Uh?" Doyle asked, sounding confused.

"What's going on?" she asked him.

"Nothing, babe. I promise I have been right in this area the entire time," replied Doyle.

"Okay. If you say so," Susan said, sitting beside him.

Doyle looked at her, "Well, that's good to know you believe me. But, hey, I just got a strange message from Leon. He said we must catch a plane and fly to California as soon as possible."

"Why? I thought we weren't going for a few more weeks?" she asked.

Doyle shook his head, "We were not supposed to. But I guess something has changed. Leon said not to worry about packing anything and that he'll deliver anything we need."

"That's nice of him," she responded.

"Yeah. I guess we need to head to Andrews Air Force Base to catch a flight," Doyle told her as he stood up.

"What about your dad? Are you going to call him and let him know you are going out early?" asked Susan.

"No. As Dad said, he is heading out on a hunting trip, and I don't want to worry him about it. All he needs is to try and remember stuff while he's hunting. I'll call him once he gets home," Doyle explained.

Susan stood up and put her arm around Doyle, "Sounds good, babe."

"I already called for a car to pick us up at the cemetery's main gate," Doyle told her as they started walking.

"How was your chat with the General?" she asked.

Doyle shrugged. "It was okay, I guess. It'll probably take me a few days to digest everything, but it was good."

"He seemed a little strange to me," she told him, grabbing and holding his hand as they walked.

"Well, he is over a hundred years old. So, he's earned the right to be a little strange. Don't you think?" Doyle asked.

Susan laughed, "Of course he has."

The couple followed the path back out of Arlington National Cemetery towards the main entrance. The General sat on a bench a few hundred yards away, watching them through binoculars.

"See? I told you he would work out just how we planned," the General said to an invisible soldier beside him.

"Yes, I see. But I still don't care for the man very much," the invisible soldier replied.

The General turned and looked at the space on the bench, "It is time you got over your hatred for him. Do I make myself clear?"

"Yes, sir," replied the soldier.

"Besides, we still have to deal with the Senator," the General said, then turned and returned the binoculars to his eyes to watch Doyle exit the cemetery.

Doyle's phone started ringing as Doyle and Susan climbed into the car to ride to Andrews Air Force Base. "This is Doyle," he said.

"Doyle, this is Leon here. I have you two on a flight lined up out of Andrews. It's a military hop, so I hope that's not a problem."

"Shouldn't be as long as it's not a C-130," Doyle responded.

Leon laughed, "What's wrong, buddy? I thought you loved those C-130 flights out of Afghanistan?"

"You know I did. I loved the netting we had to sit in," Doyle said, looking at Susan.

"That was the life, uh? Don't worry. It's on a C-17 Globemaster, and you both have seats alongside one hundred and fifty pissed-off Marines heading to Camp Pendleton," replied Leon.

"That sounds fun, thanks," Doyle responded.

"Anything for you, my friend," smirked Leon.

"Why the rush to get me out there?" asked Doyle

"I can't say over the phone, but Mike will brief you when you land at Edwards Air Force Base. After that, give me a call. You know the drill. I've arranged for Susan to stay in California while you're gone."

"Roger that," replied Doyle as he ended the call.

```
1600 HOURS * PACIFIC TIME
PRESENT-DAY
UNDERGROUND BASE-EDWARDS
```

"Come on in, Mike. No need to knock on my door," Jonah told him as he motioned for him to enter.

"I won't enter without knocking, and you know that," Mike replied.

"Nonsense. That is why I have a glass door. I finished my report on the 1895 novel by H.G. Wells, The Time Machine. I believe he was one of the forefathers of our work here. Anyway, I'm teaching a class down on level C to a group of eight-year-old future scientists. Their minds will just amaze you," Jonah explained.

Mike rolled his eyes, "That sounds boring."

"Oh, now, Mike. You should stop by sometime. I think you would enjoy it."

"I'll check my schedule. Doyle will touch down here in roughly four hours. How do you plan to get him and me to Wisconsin without being detected?" Mike asked.

Jonah smiled, then asked, "Have you ever flown in one of our flying discs?"

"Can't say that I have," Mike replied.

"That is how I plan on doing it, Mike. They are almost undetectable by radar, and they are the fastest thing we have, and the invisibility helps tremendously," Jonah told him.

Mike sat down in Jonah's chair, "I just assumed we'd go by train."

"No. All five are out and won't return in time for this mission. Plus, we need to start showing Doyle our toys and what he can use to help with his assignments," explained Jonah.

"What about Harold and Stella? We don't want them to see it, do we?" Mike asked.

"They won't. Stella and Harold will return to the train if everything goes to plan. You and Doyle will fly back in the disc," Jonah said as he typed on his computer.

"You do remember that I have an inner ear condition, right? So flying is not always good for me," Mike replied, leaning forward in his chair.

Jonah looked up and rubbed his neck, "Yes, Mike, I do. These flying discs are not like flying in an airplane or helicopter. How can I explain this without giving away any secrets?" Jonah asked himself before continuing. "You will be seated in the center of the craft, and that section has its own atmosphere. The speed and movement of

these flying discs are so extreme that a human being cannot withstand the pressure. So, we built them so you will be in a cocoon-type area. I can't go into much more detail, but trust me, you will not feel any movement."

"That's good to know," Mike said, looking more at ease.

Jonah leaned forward, "The only issue is...Time, as you know, might be somewhat blurred until you sleep it off."

"What? Like jet lag?" Mike asked.

"Yeah. You could say that," Jonah replied, smiling.

"I did say that," snapped Mike.

"You must be careful where you guys land in Wisconsin," explained Jonah.

Mike looked concerned, "What do you mean?"

Jonah laughed, "Have you ever watched the old Star Trek movies?"

"Yeah. What is your point, smart-ass?" Mike asked.

"The disc is going to land in stealth mode. It will be completely invisible, but you and Doyle won't be. Because as soon as you step out of the disk, you lose the stealth cover provided by the disk. Since you or Doyle have not been fitted for one of our suits, you must ensure nobody sees you. So, make sure you have clothes on," Jonah replied, laughing.

Mike shook his head, "I knew I should have shot you when I had the chance."

The two men's laughter echoed through the hallway of the underground base.

Harold and Stella nap while traveling underground on the high-speed rail.

Doyle and Susan arrive at Andrews Air Force Base.

CHAPTER SIX

WHEELS-DOWN /
WHEELS-UP

A cool spring breeze blows hard as two small jets land at a small regional airport near Baraboo, Wisconsin. Snow lines the rolling hills as far as the eye can see. "Close the hangar door," an FBI agent shouts after the two small jets pull inside.

"Sir. Your SUV is ready," the agent said to the Senator as he climbed down the jet's steps.

"Thank you. Have Mr. Anderson delivered to my ranch," the Senator replied, then turned toward the hangar's door. He stopped and pointed at the second jet, "Just watch that old man. He is full of surprises."

The FBI agent laughed, "I've dealt with tougher men before."

"I doubt that," The Senator said, then slammed the exit door of the hangar.

Light snow starts to fall as he walks towards his ride. Two black SUVs await the Senator. "Sir. Would you like to go straight to the ranch this evening?" asked another FBI agent.

"No. I want to stop by the Hacker-House restaurant in Baraboo first, then the ranch." The Senator climbed in the back seat of the first SUV, followed by three members of his security detail. He stared out the window for a few minutes, then turned to the man seated in the back with him, "Tony. I think I'm going to retire. I've had enough of the games. I want to finish our business here in Wisconsin, then transfer the operation away from the ranch."

"It would be hard to transfer operations without being noticed. But I will start making arrangements. Who are you going to move it to?" Tony asked.

"That I do not know yet," the Senator replied, looking out the window as the SUV pulled out of the airport. "It will probably be another Congressman; at least fifteen wanted to get in on the business."

Inside the hangar, two FBI agents walk Barry off the second jet. "Remove that bag from his head," a third agent snapped.

Barry blinked rapidly, trying to adjust his eyes to the light, "Where am I?"

"Welcome to Wisconsin, Barry. When we get outside, you'll want to take a good look around. Wisconsin will be the last state you visit," the agent replied.

"Of course. I should have known Senator Douglas would set up camp near one of the most corrupt cities in America, Madison, Wisconsin," Barry said, smiling at the agent.

"Keep on smiling, old man. We are going to enjoy wiping that off your face," one of the other agents snapped.

"If I had a dollar for every time I've heard that for fifty years. I'd be rich," Barry said to himself, then turned to one of the agents. "Can you remove these cuffs?"

"Shut it, old man," the agent replied, pushing Barry towards the exit.

The agents rush Barry to the remaining SUV and force him into the back seat. One climbs into the back seat with Barry while the other agents enter the front. They quickly speed off and out onto the I-94 ALT, heading south. They drive for five miles before turning off onto County Road W.

"Oh, I see. So, we are heading to Devil's Lake State Park, eh?" Barry asked.

The agent sitting in the back with Barry asked, "What's up with the eh?"

"That is how they talk up here in Wisconsin. Don't you DC swamp rats know anything," said Barry, shaking his head.

"Keep on talking, old man." replied the agent.

They come to a steel gate with security cameras on both sides of the road. The driver pressed a button on his sunshade, and the gate slowly lifted. The SUV drove through the gate and onto the top of a cattle road grate. The driver pressed another button on the sunshade, and the grate began to sink the SUV into an underground tunnel.

After they pulled off the grate, Barry laughed, "Well, isn't this fancy, boys."

The driver switched on the SUV's headlights and continued driving into the tunnel. The agent beside Barry pulled his handgun from his jacket pocket and hit Barry in the head…

"Sir, are you going inside the restaurant, or do you want us to pick up something for you?" the FBI agent asked Senator Douglas as they pulled into the restaurant's parking lot.

"I'm not here to eat. I have a debt to collect. So you guys stay put; I'll be right back," the Senator said, climbing out of the SUV.

"Yes, Sir." the agent replied.

"Senator Douglas, I didn't know you were in town," the restaurant's owner said when he saw the Senator walk through the door.

The Senator laughed, "Mr. Hacker, since when do I report to you?"

The owner nervously wiped his hands on his apron, "No, you do not answer to me. Of course not; I was just getting ready to call you."

"Hacker. Do you have somewhere we could talk in private?" the Senator asked, placing his arm on his shoulder.

"Yes, yes. Umm, we can go into my office."

The two walk into his small office as Hacker whispers to one of the waitresses, "Do not let anyone disturb us." She shakes her head, staring at the Senator's face. "No. I will make sure you are not bothered."

The Senator walks behind the owner's desk and takes a seat. After the owner closes the office door, the Senator motions for him to take a seat.

"Mr. Hacker. I understand you hired one of my girls for a night of pleasure. Is that correct?"

"Yy..yes, Sir." the owner answered.

The Senator leaned back in the chair, "Do you know how long I have been running this operation? Don't answer; just listen. I have been doing this since the 1980s when I took it over from a popular politician. Who, I add, had to give it up when he became President. So, let me ask you. What is my policy for payment for one of my prostitutes?"

"It is five hundred up front and one thousand after the services are complete," the owner sheepishly replied.

"Which one did you forget?" asked the Senator.

"The completion fee, Sir."

"That's correct, Mr. Hacker. Now listen. You wanted to get in this game to help your political aspirations. So, I let you in the game, but you can't follow the rules."

Mr. Hacker drops his head, "I know that I screwed up. The restaurant has not been doing well at all."

"Then maybe you should refrain from sex until you have the money," the Senator replied, then pulled his cell phone from his shirt pocket and pressed a button. "Tony, I need you in the back office."

The Senator returned his phone to his pocket, "Mr. Hacker, Tony is going to have a few words with you. Then, tomorrow, you will hand deliver me two thousand dollars. Is that understood?"

"Yes. I will get you the money. Thank you," the owner replied.

The Senator walked to the office door, "Very well. Oh, by the way. One of my men will stop by your house to give your wife pictures of you and the young lady in the Milwaukee hotel room," he said, leaving the office.

As the Senator exited the restaurant, he met Tony walking in. "Sir, what is the issue?" Tony asked.

"Mr. Hacker is in the back office awaiting you. I want you to break his right arm," the Senator replied.

Tony looked towards the back of the restaurant, "Yes, Sir."

The C-17 Globemaster sat in the late afternoon diming sunlight as the soldiers boarded with their packs. Doyle and Susan climbed up the stairs, holding each other's hands. They entered the plane and turned to walk down the aisle as an airman met them.

"Good evening, Sergeant Anderson."

Doyle nodded his head, "How are you? Please, call me Doyle."

"Yes, Sir," the airman replied, motioning for Doyle and Susan to follow him toward the middle of the plane.

"Here you go, Sir. You have an entire row to yourself." the airman said to Doyle.

"Thank you," replied Doyle.

"Sir, if you need anything, just let me know."

Doyle looked at the airman's rank on his uniform, "Thank you, Lieutenant."

Susan walked to the center of the row as Doyle followed her. Before taking their seats, he removed his backpack, pulled out his headphones and laptop, and stuffed the pack underneath the seat.

"I wonder what Leon has up his sleeve?" Susan asked.

"Not sure. I would say it's urgent to fly us out there right away."

Susan looked at him, "You should get some rest then, babe. There's no telling what he'll have you do when we land. I don't want you not to be on top of your game. You're not a young man anymore."

"Thanks for reminding me," Doyle said, putting on his reading glasses. "I'm just going to read over this case file for the search in the Crazy Mountains, and then I'll rest."

"Well. I will take advantage of the flight time and get some sleep," Susan said as the plane started taxing towards the runway.

She notices how young the soldiers in the row just in front are and remembers Doyle looking that young when he deployed years ago. She closes her eyes as the plane speeds down the runway. It lifts off the ground, vibrating and shaking as she feels the wheels retract.

After the plane reached its cruising altitude, Doyle turned his laptop on and read the file. He noticed many of the same events as other cases that led to the missing person—for example, 1) hiking alone without the proper gear, 2) getting off the known trail, and having no personal locating beacon. He also noticed some unusual events that often reoccur. For example, 1) bad weather hitting the area immediately afterward, 2) search dogs being unable to track, and 3) finding articles of the lost person's clothing.

Doyle looked up from the laptop, raised his glasses, and rubbed his eyes. Opening his eyes, he noticed a man sitting beside him. The man was in his sixties, wearing a black suit and a black fedora hat.

"Holy shit!" Doyle exclaimed as he jerked in his seat. "I didn't hear you walk up."

"I'm sorry for startling you, Doyle," the man said as he removed his hat.

"Who are you, and what can I help you with?" asked Doyle.

The man laid his hat on his lap and looked around Doyle at Susan. "She is fast asleep."

"She is. But you didn't answer my question. So, what can I help you with?" Doyle asked again.

"Don't worry. Susan will sleep until our conversation is complete," the man said with a smile.

Doyle reached under his left arm and touched the handle of his 9mm. "I'm not going to ask you again," he said.

The man grumbled, "You are not crazy enough to shoot a weapon aboard this plane."

"No one said I was going to fire it. So instead, I'm going to pistol whip the shit out of you," snapped Doyle.

"I'm here in place of Colonel Miller to speak with you. So, just relax, and we'll talk," the man responded.

"Miller? Miller is dead," Doyle said.

"He is a lot of things. But dead is not one of them. You know that, Doyle. He called you not so long ago," the man replied, smiling again.

Doyle turned toward the man, "You have your information wrong. I haven't spoken with Miller in some time."

The man nodded, "If that's how you want it. Miller did not send me here to debate with you when the last time you two spoke was. However, he sent me here to tell you he is willing to help you rescue your dad."

"Rescue my dad? What does that mean?" asked Doyle, sitting up straight in his chair.

The man looked Doyle in his eyes and asked, "So, you are not aware that the Senator has kidnapped your dad?"

"Kidnapped?" snapped Doyle.

"Yes. Senator Douglas had your dad detained and taken to an undisclosed location."

Doyle looked around the inside of the plane, then back at the man. "Let me get this straight. You are telling me that the Senator has kidnapped my dad, and I have not been made aware of this. Maybe that's because you are making this up."

The man reached into his jacket pocket, pulled out a phone, and then played a video of Barry restrained in the back of a vehicle. As he showed it to Doyle, he whispered, "Maybe I am not making this up. Eh?"

Doyle again touched his pistol. The man reached over and grabbed his hand, "Before you do something foolish, let me explain how I can help you."

Doyle relaxed his arm away from the pistol, "Tell me what you have."

"So, let me explain who I am. I worked for Miller and the Senator for more than fifteen years. I was the guy who cleaned up their messes. I created cover stories to prevent the public from seeing behind the veil. In fact, I have been misleading the people of this country ever since the 1990s," explained the mystery man.

Doyle looked at him and asked, "You are ex-military?"

The man laughed, "Heavens no. I'm a journalist for the DC Journal. I did not hear from Colonel Miller for months after the incident in California. Honestly, I thought he was dead. Then, one day, out of the blue, he called me at the Journal. The connection was terrible, all these loud squills and pops. Miller wanted me to start releasing stories about the Senator and child trafficking," he explained to Doyle.

"Incident in California?" asked Doyle, acting like he knew nothing.

The man flipped to a photo on his phone and showed it to Doyle, "I believe this is you, with an injured leg, boarding a helicopter. I know you were there during Miller's accident."

"Sorry, that's classified," Doyle said.

"If you let me continue, I'll explain why I'm here. Before publishing my story about the Senator in the Journal, Miller called again," the man said.

"And?" asked Doyle.

The man leaned forward in his seat, "He told me that he knew the Senator was planning to kidnap your dad and set him up for the child trafficking he was running. Somehow, the Senator caught wind of Miller's plan to release that information."

"That no good sum-bitch," whispered Doyle.

"Miller told me that he would notify me as soon as the kidnapping plot went into action. I was then to come to you and make you his offer," the man explained to Doyle.

"What is the offer?" Doyle asked.

The man looked at Doyle, "He will help you access the Senator's ranch in Wisconsin. What that means is that he'll help you to get around all the security systems that are in place on that ranch. So you see, the Senator is setting a trap for you. He understands that you will be coming there to rescue your dad. So the Senator will allow you access to one part of the ranch that will put you right where he wants you."

The man reached into his jacket pocket and pulled out an envelope, "This paper will give you all the codes to the sensors located throughout the ranch. There is just one catch, Mr. Anderson."

Doyle grabbed the envelope, "Yeah, and what is that?"

"You are not to kill the Senator. Just rescue your dad and then leave," The man replied.

"I don't know what to think, to be honest with you…I don't think I got your name," Doyle said to the man.

The man placed his hat on his head, "Cigar-Man, that is my name. You look over that paper, Mr. Anderson, and think about it. Just remember, do not kill him."

"And if I decide to go along with this plan, how do I let you know?" asked Doyle.

Cigar-Man smiled, "You don't contact anyone. You just do it. Because if you do not go along with it, you and your dad will never leave that ranch alive."

Doyle looked up, "I am not the type of guy that takes threats very well, Mr. Cigar-Man."

"No threat meant, Mr. Anderson. You should catch up on sleep before you land in California," he said as he side-stepped out of the aisle.

Before Doyle could reply, everything went dark.

"Well, well, well. Barry, it looks like you bumped your head. You okay, old man?"

Barry slowly opened his eyes. Looking through the bars of a cell, he saw Senator Douglas standing there smiling. "Who hit me?"

"No one hit you, Barry. They told me you tripped and fell," replied the Senator.

Barry rolled onto his back and stared at the roof above the cell, "Yeah, right. One of your damn yes-boys hit me."

The Senator leaned beside the cell close to Barry, "You just relax. Then, when Doyle arrives to try and rescue you, I will let you watch my men kill him. Then, it'll just be me and you. I will hang you in this cell and then expose to the world all of your wrongdoings. Hell, Barry, I'm even going to blame you for kidnapping all of these girls."

The Senator then held up a notepad, "This suicide note you wrote before you hung yourself explains everything."

"I didn't write shit, asshole," Barry snapped.

"Of course you did. It says right here how you regret starting this operation of child sex trafficking and how you used the mountains of North Carolina and Tennessee to kidnap these young girls," the Senator replied, smiling at Barry.

"You son-of-a-bitch," Barry shouted as he rolled over to get on his feet.

Holding a baseball bat in his left hand, the Senator stuck it into the cell and struck Barry on the head.

Barry collapsed to the floor and felt the blood run down the back of his head.

"Come on, boys. We have to get ready for Doyle to come to the rescue," the Senator said, walking toward the ramp leading out of the tunnel.

The men followed the Senator with the sound of their boots echoing off the metal ramp throughout the tunnel system. Barry squirms around until he feels the bars against his back. He grabs ahold of one and pulls himself up to a sitting position. He feels a small hand touch him on the shoulder.

"Are you okay, mister?" a soft female voice asked.

"Yeah. I'll be okay," Barry responded, rubbing his head.

The young girl sits down in her adjacent cell off to Barry's left, "We don't normally get men here."

Barry turned to her, "What do you mean by that?"

"Here in camp purgatory. It's always girls and women," she responded.

"Camp purgatory? What is that?" Barry asked.

The girl turned her head and whispered, "That is what they call it here."

Barry noticed the young woman had a black eye and a swollen lip, "What happened to you, sweetie?"

"My job the other night was for this big-time preacher, and he was the kind of man that liked to hit and beat up girls," she said, looking down at the floor.

Barry slid closer, "What do you mean your job?"

"We work for the Senator. We please significant people for him, and he rewards us with the ability to see the sun and feel the breeze on our face," the young woman explained.

Barry looked around, "Who are we?"

The lady pointed in the opposite direction. Barry turned around, and as far as he could see, there were cells with women and young girls looking toward him.

"What in the hell," he said, standing up.

"A lot of those girls were born here. Some just arrived this week," the young woman said to Barry.

Barry stood up and grabbed the bars of his cell, "Holy shit! I've searched for this place for years. I always thought it was in the Tennessee mountains."

"Tennessee is where I'm from," the woman replied, then continued. "I was on a trip to the Smoky Mountains with my girlfriends. We

had rented a cabin to celebrate and party for finally graduating from high school. I walked outside one night to smoke a cigarette when something invisible grabbed me. I can remember moving through the treetops before I blacked out. I woke up here a week later."

Barry kneeled back down, reached through the bars, and touched the woman on her shoulder, "I'm going to get you and all the girls out of here."

She looked at him and asked, "How will you do that?"

"That I do not know just yet," he replied as he looked down the tunnel and all the cages.

2117 HOURS
PRESENT-DAY
EDWARDS AIR FORCE BASE, CALIFORNIA

Doyle jumped and looked at Susan as the plane landed hard on the runway, "Oh man, I was out."

"You sure were, honey. You were snoring loudly," Susan replied.

Doyle looked around, "Did you see a man with a fedora hat on?"

"No. Why?"

"After you fell asleep, a man sat down and talked with me for a few minutes. He said that Senator Douglas had kidnapped my dad," Doyle explained.

"What?"

"That's what he said. He also said they took Dad to the Senator's ranch in Wisconsin and that I was only to rescue Dad and not touch the Senator. The man said Miller sent him," explained Doyle.

Doyle and Susan sit and stare at each other.

The plane slows down and turns towards the hangars.

Jonah watches from the top of one of the hangars at the base.

CHAPTER SEVEN
FLIGHT PLAN

The moonlight reflects off the shiny black paint of the SUV that screeches to a halt at the stairs leading to the aircraft that just arrived at Edwards. Doyle Anderson, a man with a deep-seated grudge against Jonah, stands at the top of the steps, his eyes burning with fury at the sight of the SUV. With an unmistakable smirk, Jonah, a man who exudes confidence, steps out of the vehicle, his confidence radiating like a forcefield.

"Damn you, Jonah, you knew I would have never flown here if you had told me that the Senator has my dad," Doyle erupted, his voice quivering with a shock that reverberated through the air as he descended the steps with a clenched fist. The revelation of his father's capture by the Senator, a man Doyle has long despised, has set his heart ablaze with a fury he can barely contain.

With his hands raised in a gesture of peace, Jonah steps back as Doyle approaches, his voice steady and composed. "Now, just calm down, Doyle. If I had told you, you would have rushed off in all your anger and fury. Then the Senator would have killed you and Barry."

Doyle, consumed by his anger, lunges toward Jonah, a move that could escalate the situation. In a display of his physical prowess, Jonah swiftly grabs Doyle and pins him back first onto the hood of the SUV. "If you allow me to train you in patience, you will be unstoppable," he asserts, hinting at a deeper strategy involving more than just brute force and anger.

"Let me up," Doyle grunts as Jonah releases him. "Why didn't you allow me to go straight to Wisconsin?"

Jonah looks at the top of the stairs as Susan watches the events below. "Because it would have jeopardized our entire operation. And she more than likely would have been killed," he said, pointing at Susan.

Doyle turned and looked up at his wife, Susan, then lowered his head in embarrassment, his face flushed with shame. "Yeah, I guess you are correct, Jonah," he admitted, his voice filled with resignation and regret.

"Your passion makes you great, but it can also be your greatest weakness. We are not only fighting with Senator Douglas and the Shadow Government but also with powerful spiritual entities you cannot see," explained Jonah, revealing a hidden layer of the conflict that Doyle was unaware of.

"I don't understand?" Doyle replied.

"I believe you do, Doyle; you just don't want to accept what you've always known to be fact. But we will have plenty of time to discuss that after we rescue your Dad. We have to get Susan to a safe location, and you and Mike will fly out to Wisconsin before the sun rises."

When the SUV's back door opens, Mike Rosen, Doyle's partner from the dangerous mission in California last year, climbs out. "I'm no more excited about us working together again than you are, Doyle," Mike tells him.

"Mike, good to see you again," Doyle said as he walked over to shake Mike's hand.

Observing the scene as she descended the stairs, Susan walked over to Doyle and firmly placed her arm around him. "I want to go with my husband. I can't bear the thought of him facing this alone," she declared, her voice filled with unwavering determination. Her eyes, filled with a fierce resolve, met Jonah's, silently challenging him to deny her request.

"We cannot allow that, Susan. It will be too dangerous, plus we do not have room in the aircraft they are taking. You will be most comfortable here and very safe. Mike and Doyle will not be gone more than six hours, so you will hardly know they are gone before they are back," Jonah explained.

"Are we going to stand here blubbering like a bunch of schoolgirls, or are we going to get going?" Mike asked.

"Susan, this is Mike. The nicest horses-ass you'll ever meet," Doyle said to her.

Susan smiled and shook Mike's hand. " It's Nice to meet you. I've heard nothing but good things about you."

"Okay. Everybody in the vehicle, we must get going," Jonah said as he motioned for them to enter the SUV.

The SUV speeds away from the idle aircraft, its powerful engine roaring across the dried lake bed. Once a thriving body of water, the landscape is now a barren desert stretching out in all directions. In the distance, a top-secret hangar, a massive structure hidden beneath the desert sands, comes into view. Its entrance is guarded by armed personnel and high-tech security systems, a testament to the importance of what lies within.

2 145 HOURS
PRESENT-DAY
THE PATRIOTS GROUP UNDERGROUND TRAIN DEPOT.
WISCONSIN

Stella senses the train abruptly halting, followed by a series of unsettling bounces as it is lifted from the underground tunnel. They have arrived at the destination.

"Welcome to Wisconsin, Stella and Harold," Jonah says from the intercom in their cabins.

"I will give you both a crucial wake-up call at 0330 hours, and then at 0400 hours, a pivotal moment will arrive when one of my security

guards will board the train. Both of you must be prepared," Jonah's voice resonates from the intercom in their cabins.

"Can we get something to eat before we turn in?" asked Harold.

"Both of your cabin doors are unlocked now, and there is a full kitchen with everything you need in front of the large conference room you entered earlier," Jonah replied.

"Okay. Thank you, Jonah," Stella said as she opened the door to her cabin. She walked into the conference room only to see Harold beat her out there. Harold was rummaging through the refrigerators, looking for the right thing to hit the spot.

"Are you that hungry, Harold?" she asked.

"I am starving," he answered with a carrot sticking out of his mouth.

The intercom crackles, "You two will still not be permitted to exit the train; you can move freely between your cabins and the conference room. But, as I said, you both need sleep. 0330 hours will come early," warned Jonah.

"I-Captain," Stella joked with him.

"Goodnight, you two," Jonah said as the intercom clicked off.

"Harold, did you learn anything interesting about the Senator's security system at the ranch from the video?" she asked.

Harold sat his cup down and looked at her with a milk ring on his top lip. "It is a fairly old system and easy to bypass. I'm shocked by

the Senator's business: he doesn't have a more sophisticated system. You should try some of this milk; it is wonderful," he replied, taking another drink.

Stella laughed and shook her head, "You need a paper towel; you have a milk mustache."

They chuckled, relishing their late-night snack. "Just like the good old days, huh, Harold?" Stella remarked with a hint of nostalgia in her voice.

"We are old," Harold responded.

They both laughed uncontrollably.

2200 HOURS
PRESENT-DAY
THE SENATOR'S RANCH, WISCONSIN

Barry, a late-aged man with a rugged face and a gray beard, slowly opens his eyes. He had drifted off in a short nap after the brutal hit to his head, a blow that had left him disoriented and in pain. He sees the young woman, a girl in her late teens, looking at him with a determined look in her eyes. "Are you okay?" she asks, her voice filled with concern.

"I think so, honey. My head is pounding like a drum," Barry groaned, his voice strained with the pain from the hit to his head. He leaned forward onto his knees, gripping one of the cold, iron cell bars, and pulled himself up. The area was shrouded in darkness, with

just a few dim lights barely illuminating the walkways through the underground prison, casting eerie shadows on the damp stone walls.

"So, do you have a plan to get us all out of here? There are more than twenty of us here; we have had three die recently from complications of different types of diseases," the young girl said with pain in her voice.

Barry looked out of his cell and into the darkness, "No, I do not have a plan, but when they come back here, you just follow my lead. We'll fight to get us all out of here." His voice, filled with a steely determination, echoed through the dimly lit prison, instilling a glimmer of hope in the hearts of his fellow prisoners.

"We will help any way we can. I know where all the exits are and the times the guards change shifts," the young girl told Barry, her voice filled with a quiet determination that belied her age.

Barry nodded his head, "That'll help, sweetie. But, unless we figure a way out of these cages, I'm afraid it won't be much help to us."

The young girl sat there, picking the skin on her neck, "I know how we can get out."

"How is that?"

She started digging at the dirt floor, her small hands covered in grime. "The short guard always comes by and gets me out of the cage every night at midnight. He says he likes talking to me and that I remind him of his sister. Cold and damp dirt floor clung to her fingers as she dug, creating a small mound of earth beside her.

"He doesn't hurt you, does he?" Barry asked.

"No. The short guard is one of the nice ones. He made me swear I'd never tell because the Senator would have him killed if he knew. We just talk, and he lets me have a soft drink because the Senator never allows us to have those," she said, hinting at a secret that could change their fate.

Barry turns his back to her, his face contorted with anger and determination, "She is just a child. I will hurt the Senator when I get my hands on him." His voice, filled with rage and protectiveness, resonated through the dimly lit prison.

"Did you say something?" she asked.

"No, sweetie. I was just thinking out loud. Do you think he will still come and get you with me here?" Barry asked, his voice filled with concern.

"Yes, but only if you are asleep. At ten thirty, the guards will put tarps over our cages so we can't see each other or whatever happens at night in here. I can try to get his keys if you want me to."

"Let me think about it for a few minutes. I don't want you getting hurt, sweetie." Barry told her as he slid down the bars, the cold metal biting into his skin, sitting on the damp ground with a concerned look.

2230 HOURS
PRESENT-DAY
JONAH'S OFFICE, UNDERGROUND BASE, CALIFORNIA

Doyle, a restless agent, sits in one of the office chairs in Jonah's office, his leg bouncing with nervous energy as he swiftly flips through one of his notebooks. Mike, his seasoned partner, sits on the other side of the office, his gaze fixed on Doyle, a hint of amusement in his eyes. "Are you going to wet your pants?" Mike teases Doyle, his voice laced with a mix of concern and jest.

Doyle looks at Mike over his reading glasses, "I'll be fine, old man."

Mike laughs, "You look like a child waiting in the principal's office after he got caught smoking in the boy's room. You always get so nervous before a mission, don't you?"

Doyle laid his notebook down, reached into his shirt pocket, removed a cigar, lit it, and leaned back into the chair. "This better, Mike?"

"Much better, smart ass."

Doyle smiled a mischievous glint in his eyes, with the cigar clenched in his teeth.

The office door abruptly opened, and Jonah walked in. As he passed Doyle, he grabbed the cigar out of his mouth and threw it into the trash can. "Don't smoke that in here, Doyle."

Mike let out a laugh.

"Hey," Doyle exclaimed as he leaned forward and pulled the cigar from the trash, "These things are not cheap!" he snapped.

Jonah sits at his desk, "You'll be happy to know that my men have transported Susan to a safe location within the underground base. She will have a nice meal and shower before they show her to her quarters for the night."

"Thank you for that," responded Doyle.

"Okay. We must prepare both of you to embark on a mission of utmost secrecy to Wisconsin. It's your lucky day, Doyle. You and Mike will board one of our flying disks, a technology so advanced and classified that it's as if it doesn't exist according to our government," Jonah reveals to Mike, his voice tinged with a hint of excitement and mystery.

Knowing that Harold and Stella will arrive at the Senators' ranch at 0730 hours central time, Jonah cannot have Doyle and Mike on the ground there before that. "This disk is not just any aircraft; it's a high-speed marvel. It will whisk you from here to there in a mere forty-five minutes. So, you will need to rest, and we will reconvene at 0400 hours, with a departure time of 0500 hours," Jonah explains, adding a thrilling element to the mission.

"What is a flying disk?" asked Doyle.

"I'm sure you have seen pictures of it in the newspapers or TV. It is a reverse-engineered aircraft from one that crashed many years ago," replied Jonah. The flying disk is a top-secret government project that

harnesses advanced alien technology, making it capable of unparalleled speed and maneuverability.

"What, a UFO?"

"Yes, Doyle. If you want to use that phrase, a UFO." Jonah said with a coy smile.

Doyle just looked at Jonah, "Okay."

Jonah turned his chair around, facing the back wall of his office. He pressed a button, and the back wall slowly rose, unveiling a picture glass window overlooking a vast hangar below. The round flying disk sat in the heart of the hangar, a sight that left Doyle in awe. Men moved around it, performing checks with laptops. Doyle stood and walked to the glass, his breath catching in his throat as he stared, unable to tear his eyes away from the magnificent sight.

"That is the coolest thing I've ever seen," Doyle exclaimed, his eyes widening with awe as he gazed at the futuristic aircraft.

Jonah stood up beside Doyle, "You have not seen anything yet."

Doyle stands there just watching the men moving around below when a bright light flashes, triggering his PTSD.

1030 HOURS
13 DECEMBER 1987
WORLD TRADE CENTERS NEW YORK CITY

"Slow down, dude!" John Miller (Colonel Miller), a tall, skinny man with a perpetual smirk, yells to Doyle. "I told her we would be

at the South Tower at 1030, and it's already 1030," Doyle, a wiry man with a perpetual frown, says, running up the steps from the subway. Doyle tops the steps and goes out of site. He meets Susan, and they watch John and Aaron (Bullseye's brother) from their hiding spot.

"We are not running, Aaron. We'll meet up with them when we get there," Miller says.

"Okay," Aaron, a young man with a perpetual look of confusion, replies.

"That boy is not thinking straight," Miller says, elbowing Aaron.

"He just likes her; that's all, John."

"Call me Miller; I don't like the name John."

"Okay. I don't like being called my last name, Williams. I like Aaron better," Aaron tells him.

They both step outside the subway stairs and stop dead in their tracks. "Holy shit!" Aaron exclaims.

"Wow," responds Miller as they both stare up at the

World Trade Center towers.

"How can someone build something this tall?" Aaron asks.

"I don't know, but it looks like they are swaying with the clouds moving behind them," Miller tells him.

"Yeah, it's almost making me seasick," Aaron says, pulling a disposable camera from his pocket. He starts taking pictures as they continue walking to find Doyle.

As soon as they start walking, Doyle and Susan jump out and shout, "Freeze, this is a hold-up!" "Hilarious guys, sneaking up on us like that," Miller says to them. "What do you mean I'm not thinking straight?" Doyle asks Miller.

"Someone could get hurt doing that in the city," explains Miller.

"Y'all didn't scare me," Aaron tells Susan.

"Okay. I'm sorry, it was Doyle's idea. Hey, let's have lunch on the 107th-floor food court," Susan suggests, her voice filled with anticipation. The idea immediately sparks interest in the group.

"That sounds cool," replies Doyle, his voice filled with eagerness.

"I'll pay for everyone," Miller says as they walk into the majestic South Tower and up to the booth to pay. "They'll be four for the observation deck," says Miller to the lady working the booth, her face framed by the booth's glass window.

"That's four tickets to the Top of the World," the lady says, handing him four tickets and his change with a smile.

"Thanks. Hey, what time do you get off work?" Miller asks the lady, his eyes twinkling mischievously.

"I'm sorry, ma'am," Doyle says, pushing Miller away from the window.

"What? It would have been worth her time. Did you see her rack?" Miller asks Doyle with a playful grin.

"Just keep walking, big mouth," replies Doyle, his voice tinged with exasperation.

"Maybe next time!" Miller shouts back to her as the elevator doors close, his voice echoing in the space.

"Oh, wow!" Aaron says as he looks out the window from the 107th floor of the Top of the World Observation Deck.

"Pretty awesome, isn't it?" Susan asks him.

"Yes, it is. We have to go up to the top after a while."

"We will," she says, grabbing Doyle's hand and looking out the window. It's a clear day with a few white clouds floating in the sky.

"Come over and look out, Miller," Doyle says.

Shaking his head, Miller replied, "That's okay; I'm not crazy about heights."

Susan laughed, "What? Are you afraid you might fall?"

"Yeah, something like that," Miller replied, walking away.

The gang sits down and devours their lunch: hot dogs and fries. "I'm ready to go up to the top and see where King Kong stood," Aaron says, his voice filled with childlike excitement.

"You do know that he wasn't there, right?" Miller asks him, a hint of teasing in his voice.

"Says you," snaps Aaron, a playful challenge in his tone.

"Okay then, let's go see King Kong," Miller replies, rolling his eyes but smiling.

"Come on, Doyle, this is unbelievable," Susan says, tugging his arm.

"Alright, let's do this," he replies, putting on his military-issued sock hat with a determined look, ready for the adventure.

They ride two sets of escalators up to the top of the building and walk out onto the platform that wraps around the top of the tower. The wind is blowing with the temperature in the low forties, chilling their faces and making their hair flutter. "Oh my, it's cold up here," Susan says, snuggling up to Doyle. Aaron walks over and looks through a pair of binoculars towards the Empire State Building, "Wow! This is so awesome!" he yells back to Doyle and Susan.

"Yes, it is!" Susan yells back as she and Doyle walk to the south side of the platform. "If you look hard, that small island is the Statue of Liberty," she points to Doyle...

2230 HOURS
PRESENT-DAY
JONAH'S OFFICE. UNDERGROUND BASE. CALIFORNIA

"Doyle, are you okay?" Jonah asked, his voice laced with deep concern. His hand gently rested on Doyle's back.

"I've told you time and again, he is damaged goods!" Mike's voice rose with frustration.

Doyle's vision slowly cleared up. He turned and returned to his seat, his hand trembling as he rubbed the top of his head. He smiled: "I'm just fine, just a little tired. The jet lag is starting to set in."

Mike loomed over Doyle, his voice dripping with disdain, "That looked like more than jet lag to me. He is not capable of pulling this mission off, Jonah."

Jonah retrieved a bottle of water from a small fridge under his desk, "He will be just fine; after he gets some rest, he'll be as good as new."

"I don't think so. If Doyle has one of these attacks during our mission, he will get us killed," Mike snapped.

"I'll be okay, Mike. I've been dealing with these attacks for years now. I'm normally in bed by now, and my meds are wearing down," explained Doyle.

"He is correct, Mike. I will have one of my aids show both of you to your quarters now," Jonah said as he picked up a small radio and pressed the microphone. "Can we escort Mike and Doyle to their quarters now?"

A man's voice came over the radio, "10-4 Jonah, I'm on my way."

"Very good. Thank you. My assistant is on his way. I will give you both a wake-up call at 0345 hours."

"I don't know, Jonah," Mike started before Jonah cut him off.

"Just stop it, Mike. I have often explained to you how the ones with illnesses have better connections with other dimensions. We are using

Doyle, and there will be no more questions about this matter. Am I clear with you, Mike?" Jonah's voice was firm, brooking no argument.

"Yeah. We are clear. But I'm just telling you, I will not hesitate to eliminate Doyle if he risks the mission!" Mike's voice was sharp with determination.

Jonah stared at Mike, "That will not happen."

The tension in the room is thick.

Jonah's assistants escort Doyle and Mike from the office.

Jonah turned and looked at the flying disk.

INTERLUDE
THE CIGAR-MAN

2200 HOURS
PRESENT-DAY
MOJAVE DESERT, CALIFORNIA

The enigmatic figure known as the Cigar-Man, a solitary presence in the vast, desolate expanse of the Mojave desert, gazes at the distant lights of Edwards Air Force Base. The moon, a silent witness, begins its ascent from the east, casting an ethereal glow over the barren landscape, while the haunting howls of coyotes pierce the stillness of the night, adding to the eerie atmosphere.

"You did a good job. Are you certain Doyle understood our directions?" Colonel Miller's voice held a hint of respect for me, a testament to our shared history and mutual understanding.

"Yes, Colonel Miller, Doyle understood," I say as I take a long draw from my cigar. I notice the sand on the ground four feet away swirling around a few feet from the ground, and I hear Colonel Miller's voice coming from that location.

"Doyle will check to see if you work as a journalist."

"That's not a concern, Colonel. Doyle will be too consumed with rescuing his father, who he feared was long dead, to question my true identity. By the time he realizes, I'll be far away, and so will you." My voice resonated with a chilling certainty, hinting at a deeper, personal connection, instilling a sense of reassurance with Colonel Miller.

"You sound confident that Doyle will not find out you are also a time traveler," Colonel Miller said with much doubt.

"It is not essential for him to know or not to know, Colonel. He will, in time, see it for himself just as he will see that you are not of this dimension any longer."

I hear Colonel Miller laugh an eerie laugh that causes the desert to go silent, "If Doyle could see what I can, he would understand how weak and fragile he truly is."

I flicked my cigar away and, using my foot, grind it into the sand. "Colonel Miller, you need to get to Wisconsin to prepare for Doyle's arrival and the inevitable clash with Senator Douglas, a man with a secret agenda that could change the course of history. I will accompany Doyle from here and guide him to the precise location of the impending showdown."

"You do know that Dr. Furcus will work to stop us and will not rest until he has removed us from the game," Colonel Miller explained.

"He has already changed the matrix, so I cannot travel into the future. I continue to travel back in time and stay for extended periods to keep him from locating me."

I possess a unique ability to manipulate time, a power that Dr. Furcus, a rogue scientist with his own time-traveling agenda, was desperate to control. To thwart his plans, I had to constantly shift between different time periods, making it difficult for him to track my movements. After I explained this, Colonel Miller disappeared into the desert, leaving a trail of dust and many unanswered questions.

I pulled another Cigar from my pocket and lit it. I need to travel back to the construction of the Senator's ranch in the 1980s and install a bug in the software so that I can get Doyle in and allow the sniper to take the kill shot. I start walking towards the secret underground base at Edwards Air Force Base. It's just a matter of time before Jonah reaches out to me.

A falling star streaked across the lonely desert sky, a celestial omen of the impending events. A coyote approached where Colonel Miller once stood, its hair raised on its back before fleeing, a sign of the imminent danger and the animal's instinct to survive.

CHAPTER EIGHT
THE ART OF DECEPTION

The underground prison is a place of eerie silence, broken only by occasional footsteps echoing through the narrow corridors. Two guards, the short one and his taller companion, came by an hour and a half ago and placed the tarps over all the cells. The young girl, a sexual-trafficked prisoner, was awakened by the short guard touching her. "Are you up for our nightly chat?" he asked, his voice a whisper in the darkness.

She rolled over and looked at him, "Sure," she said in a low voice, her eyes betraying a hint of fear and uncertainty.

The guard, a man of few words, quietly removed his keys and pushed the tarp away to unlock and open her cage. "Shh," he said as he took her hand and helped her from the cage. They both tippy-toed down the path, past a row of other cages, and into a small storage

room. He flipped the light on and locked the door. He handed her a diet soda, "I know you have been waiting all day for this."

She reached out and took the soda, "I have, thanks."

"Something feels different tonight. I'm not sure what it is, but there is tension in the air. Have you felt the tension?" the guard asked.

"No. Everything feels the same to me, I guess."

He shook his head, "I don't know; something is happening—that man they brought in, the one in the cell next to you. I have a bad feeling about him."

"Why do you say that? He seems like a harmless old man, someone's grandfather," she replied.

"I'm not sure about him. He has this vibe like he is some mighty man. I hope he's not the President or something," he told her.

"No way. Do you think so?" she asked.

The short guard nodded, "Yes. I do. Hey, I have been thinking about getting out of here. I don't like this gig anymore. If I was to, say, break you out of here, would you go with me?"

"The Senator would hunt you down and kill you," she explained.

"He would have to find us first. I have family in Iowa, where we could hide out until the Senator thinks we left the country. What do you think? You want to break out of here?" he asked, his voice filled with determination.

"I do. But I'm terrified of what the Senator would do to us. How could we get out of here without triggering the alarms?" the young girl asked, her voice trembling with fear.

The guard sat there for a few seconds, thinking about what she had just said: "I think I know how we could get out."

The two sat staring at each other when his radio went off, "All nightshift personnel report to the cell block ASAP. We are relieved for the night."

"Oh shit! We have to get you back to your cell fast!" he urgently told her.

"Before I go, I want a hug. I have been coming with you every night for months, and you have never hugged me. And now you want me to run off with you and risk our lives," she said to him.

"Okay. I'll hug you. Just hurry up. If we get caught, we are for sure dead."

The young girl hugged him for what seemed like an eternity, and then they both quickly walked back to her cell. The guard closed and locked her cage and replaced the tarp. "I'll see you tomorrow night, okay?" he asked.

"Okay," she replied.

She heard him walk away and then reached into Barry's cell and poked him. "Well, did you have any luck?" Barry asked.

She pulled the tarp away where she could see Barry and held up the short guards' keys, "Yes," she said as she giggled.

"Great job, sweetie! Let me have them just in case he comes back looking for them. I will hide the keys under my mattress. Now, let's get some rest. We'll need it come morning," Barry told her.

"Good night," she replied.

```
03 15 HOURS * CENTRAL DAYLIGHT TIME
PRESENT-DAY
THE PATRIOTS GROUP UNDERGROUND TRAIN DEPOT.
WISCONSIN
```

In the main conference room on the train, Harold and Stella, their cups filled with the aroma of freshly brewed coffee, discuss the events that led them to this pivotal moment. The dawn of a new day, promising to alter their lives forever, looms just hours away.

"So, after you and Barry had your memories erased, how long did it take for you to realize that you still had your memory?" Harold asked, his voice laced with a hint of suspense.

Stella, her hands cradling the warm coffee cup, feels the heat seep into her aged fingers. She turns to Harold, her eyes reflecting a mix of weariness and determination, and answers, "The next day."

"Interesting. Were you worried about what the Patriot's Group would do to you if they found out?"

"No. I was worried about what General **X** might do to Barry if he found out. We are the Patriot's Group, not the leadership. It was

hard keeping it from Barry, but I knew it was best for him. But, I also knew that Barry, with all of his extensive notes, had to regain his memory and finish this fight," Stella's voice resonated with unwavering determination.

Harold's eyebrows raise in surprise, and he recalls, "Barry always kept the best notes. He is a very detailed person. He stopped by my home a few days back and showed me his journal he had dug out of the ground. He wanted me to help him regain that part of his memory."

"Yeah. I knew it was just a matter of time before Barry sought you out for help. I had that journal for many years after our group wiped his memory. I buried it in our yard, and I would whisper to him a night, as if I was the devil he chased through the Smokies, and tell him to search for it," Stella explained.

"Amazing. Girl, you are one good soldier. I never would have thought of that. Do you think Barry will ever regain his memory?" he asked.

Stella sat her coffee cup down. "To be honest, I do not. He's getting too old, and with the damage that wiping his memory caused, that damage may never be reversed," she said, her voice tinged with uncertainty, yet her spirit remained unbroken.

"Hopefully, he will regain some of his memory," Harold said as the intercom cracked.

"Rise and shine, my two fine troopers," Jonah's voice echoes throughout the train.

"We are up, Jonah," Harold responded.

"Great! I am unlocking the entrance door so that my assistant can enter and help you get your things together," Jonah told them as the door unlatching began.

"Jonah, we have our things together. I have my sniper rifle and all my gear packed into my pack," Stella, the team's sharpshooter, replied.

"I do as well," Harold chimed in.

"Perfect! Then this should go smoothly," said Jonah as a small, mysterious drone floated through the now-open train entrance. The drone, with its unknown capabilities, flew near Stella and Harold.

"Good Morning," a robotic voice said, leaving the two with more questions than answers.

"What on earth is this, Jonah?" Harold asked, his voice filled with a mix of awe and curiosity.

"This is Eddie, my drone assistant," Explained Jonah. "He's equipped with advanced surveillance systems and can assist us in various tasks, from reconnaissance to carrying our equipment."

Harold waved his arm at the drone, "I do not work with robots!"

The drone swerved to avoid getting knocked out of the sky. A small hatch opened on the drone, and a taser appeared.

"If that thing tases me, Jonah!" shouted Harold, pointing at the drone.

The sound of Jonah laughing echoes throughout the conference room, "Then I suggest you do not try to hit Eddie."

"Calm down, Harold; I'm sure it will be okay," Stella told him, her voice filled with reassurance and understanding.

"Yes, Harold, calm down. Since this underground depot is so close to the Senator's ranch, I cannot use very many actual people. So, I use drones, AI robots, and my robot owls. My robots have built-in software that can detect an invisible soldier and even jam GPS signals. You will be most happy that they are by your side for this mission," Jonah reassured him.

"If you would please gather your belongings and trust me enough to follow, we can begin," Eddie instructed, then swiftly exited through the open door, confident in Harold and Stella's ability to keep up.

Harold and Stella, stepping off the train, were immediately struck by the advanced and extensive underground depot. Seeing several drones buzzing around and at least four AI robots diligently working on a train engine in what appeared to be a maintenance shop was awe-inspiring and slightly unnerving. One of the AI robots even welded a door hinge on a separate train car. As they followed Eddie, Stella couldn't help but notice three of Jonah's robot owls perched on what seemed to be a charging stand, their metallic feathers glinting in the artificial light.

"We are transferring you to a smaller train, which travels above ground only, to the Senator's ranch. Once we arrive at the ranch, I will protect the train while the mission is ongoing," Eddie, the drone, explained as they walked through the depot.

"Harold, are we the only human beings in this place?" Stella asked.

Hearing her question, Eddie replied, "That is correct, Mrs. Anderson. The location of this depot is too close to the very political and corrupt city of Madison. The director found that having our secret operations run by robots is safer."

"Isn't Jonah worried about someone hacking the system?" she asked.

"Not at all. This system is not software-based, at least not artificial software-based," replied Eddie.

"I do not know what that means, Eddie," Stella said, shrugging her shoulders.

Eddie flies around a corner and turns back to Stella. "You are not allowed to understand."

The duo continues to follow Eddie as they encounter even more AI robots that are hard at work. They see what looks to be a sleek, black stealth helicopter sitting on a railcar, its surface reflecting the dim light of the depot. Four AI robots cover the aircraft with a camo tarp, making it nearly invisible to the naked eye.

A sliding door opens to the depot's main cafeteria, a large room adorned with elegant tablecloths and chandeliers that exude luxury.

The mirrored walls reflect the light off the floor's glass tiles, creating a grandeur that is hard to miss. "We had our chefs prepare you both an excellent breakfast. I will remain just outside the door and will come and get you at 0500 hours," explained Eddie, the drone.

Two AI chefs, efficient and precise in their movements, approach Stella and Harold. They escort the guests to their tables with attentive service. "We have everything ready for you. There is a large breakfast bar and six different types of coffee. Also, fresh Wisconsin milk," one of the AI chefs tells them.

"Thank you," replied Stella.

0430 HOURS * CENTRAL DAYLIGHT TIME
PRESENT-DAY
THE SENATOR'S RANCH, WISCONSIN

Barry reached into the young girl's cell and shook her mattress, "It's time, sweetie."

"I'm awake," she replied.

"Good. I have already been out of my cell scoping everything out. The Senator sent all the guards home earlier, which is not a good sign. If I had to guess, the Senator plans on doing something bad and doesn't want too many witnesses," Barry explained.

The young girl sat up, her voice trembling, "I was thinking the same thing. They never go home before 0800 hours. I am terrified about what might happen."

"Yeah, me too. But we have to get all the girls out of their cells quickly. I have found a good spot to hide everyone until I can figure out what to do," Barry told her as he unlocked the cage.

The girl jumped off her mattress and turned to grab her small teddy bear, which she sleeps with every night. "Okay, I'm ready."

Barry had to turn his back to keep her from seeing his eyes teared up, "Good Lord, mentally, she is just a child."

"Hand me the keys, and I'll unlock the other girl's cages if you remove the tarps," she told him, holding her hand out.

"That's a good idea. Let's do it!"

With unwavering determination, Barry quickly moved down the center between the rows of cages, pulling the tarps off as he went. Every two sets of cages, he dropped the tarps and started again; once he reached the last set of cages, he dropped the tarps and turned back to check on the young girls' progress.

By twos, the girls ran up to Barry and stood behind him as he counted them, "Okay. That is 24 girls; is that all of them?" he asked, his voice concerned for their safety.

"Yes. That is all that is left," Barry's young accomplish answered him.

"Great! Now, if all of you follow me ahead and around the curve to the left, there is a large water filtration room that we can hide in. The door opens inward so we can block it to keep anyone out. There was a

vent in the ceiling that I could see the moon through earlier tonight. I should be able to climb out that way and get help," Barry explained. The girls, their relief palpable and hope renewed, followed Barry.

As the last girl stepped into the room, Barry swiftly closed and locked the door and slid a large cabinet in front of it. "This should buy us some time while I go for help," he reassured the girls, his voice tinged with urgency.

"There's no one out there to help; the Senator has everyone in this county under his control," the young girl informed Barry, her tone confident and wise beyond her years.

Barry settled on a table, taking in the room's contents. Reverse osmosis machines, water softeners, and water heaters were scattered about, their noise creating a cacophony that masked their presence and hindered any communication within the cell block.

"We're running out of time. What's our next move?" Barry urgently asked, but he was asking himself.

"We'll go out through the roof vent and escape together," the young girl declared with unwavering determination.

Barry shook his head, "None of you have shoes or pants. You are all in your nightgowns. This ranch is rocky terrain; it'll cut your feet to pieces before we get one hundred yards. Once the Senator discovers we are all outside the tunnels, he'll release hound dogs to track us down. Plus, we don't even know what the best direction is to go."

"What are you saying then? That we all sit here and wait for the Senator to find us and punish us for leaving our cells?" the young girl asked.

Barry walked over and placed his hands on her shoulders, "I never asked you your name, sweetie."

"My name is Emily," she replied.

"Well, Emily. I think that would be best for now. I've been missing for almost twelve hours, and the group I worked for no doubt already knows where I am. They are probably already in the process of sending someone in to rescue me."

"How can you be sure they will find you?" Emily asked, her voice thick with doubt, echoing the heavy uncertainty in the room.

"Because I know the people in charge, they'll find me, and then they'll find all of you," Barry explained, his voice laced with a sense of urgency and unwavering confidence. His words were a balm to the room's uncertainty.

Emily walked away from him and looked up into the dimly lit ceiling vent. "What if the Senator finds us before your rescuers get here?"

"Then we fight," Barry declared, his voice brimming with unwavering determination.

"With what? We have no weapons or strength. The Senator only feeds us enough to keep us alive. We cannot fight and win," Emily said, her voice echoing with resignation.

"You have anger, don't you? Are you not mad about the way the Senator has treated you like a dirty animal? That alone will be enough to win. If it's not, then we fight with our minds. We outthink them if we have to. But I know there is help on the way!" Barry's voice is now rising, his confidence and determination filling the room.

"You are right. I was only thinking about getting out of this prison and not what we would do once we climbed out. We will wait for you to tell us how we fight. I never got your name, sir." Emily asked, her eagerness to learn from him shining through.

"My name is Barry. Barry Anderson."

Emily smiled. "We fight with you, Mr. Barry Anderson."

```
0505 HOURS * CENTRAL DAYLIGHT TIME
PRESENT-DAY
THE PATRIOTS GROUP UNDERGROUND TRAIN DEPOT.
WISCONSIN
```

"Oh great, there is that dang flying computer," Harold said as he and Stella exited the cafeteria.

Stella laughed, "You are a cranky old man, Harold."

"I take it your breakfast was satisfying?" Eddie asked as he flew up beside the pair.

"Yes, it was wonderful," Stella replied.

"Wonderful. We have a small hike yet to get both of you to the train we'll use for our mission," Eddie explained, emphasizing the teamwork aspect as they continued through the vast depot.

Harold looked across the way and noticed two AI robots working on an AI wolf with a laptop computer plugged into a port. "What are they doing to that robot wolf?" he asked Eddie.

"They are updating its software for our mission," responded Eddie.

"We are using a wolf?" asked Stella.

"Yes indeed. We are also using an owl and two whitetail deer; all are cutting-edge AI robotics built nearby in Milwaukee, Wisconsin," Eddie told them as he flew along, emphasizing the novelty of the technology.

Harold leaned toward Stella, "This Eddie is like the spokesman for Jonah and all his crazy gadgets."

"Jonah's gadgets are not crazy but state-of-the-art. Jonah has won many awards for his inventions," Eddie replied.

Harold looked at Stella and rolled his eyes.

As they approached the depot's exit, light rain started falling. "Eddie, what is the weather forecast today?" Stella, the team's sniper, asked.

"There is an 80 percent chance of rain until noon, then snow. The weather experts are calling for eight inches of snow by sundown," Eddie explained, his voice echoing in the cavernous depot.

Harold looked concerned, "The rain doesn't bother me, but the snow could be an issue if we run into delays getting back to the train."

"There can be no delays. My system has been informed that the Shadow Government will send reinforcements by early afternoon." As Eddie said this, the exit doors slid open, revealing the above-ground train nearby.

"We won't be delayed; we've been through this before," Stella reassured, climbing onto the train.

Harold followed suit, boarding the train. They both arranged their gear in a row of seats, then made their way to the back of the train car and took a seat. Eddie rushed through the door, which promptly closed, and the computer monitor on the front wall flickered to life.

"Good morning, crew," Jonah said as his face appeared on the monitor.

"Good morning," both Stella and Harold replied.

"There will be a small delay before we can get moving. There is train traffic on the rail this morning, and we must let the train traffic pass before we can shut the rail down. I have installed a four-hour delay on the rail this morning in the Devil's Lake area, which includes the Senator's ranch. That time should be enough for both of you to go into the ranch and out with the survivors."

"Survivors, plural?" Stella asked.

Jonah nodded, "That is correct. The Senator holds Barry in his underground prison, where he holds his sex-trafficked girls. We do not know how many prisoners there are, but it could be as many as thirty." The revelation of multiple prisoners left Stella and Harold stunned.

"I knew it!" Stella's voice rang with a triumphant note, her suspicions finally confirmed. Her eyes sparkled with the thrill of being right.

"So that we are all on the same page. You, Stella, are only allowed to take the shot at the Senator and not go into the tunnels that house the prisoners. I am sending Doyle, who will be on the ground in Wisconsin soon, to go into the prison to release the prisoners. He will then guide them to the train so that Harold can take over their escape. Most importantly, Doyle can not know that you, Stella, are present. Doyle thinks that Harold is the only one on that train," Jonah clarified, to instill confidence in the characters about their roles.

Stella nodded, "That sounds good, Jonah; I felt Doyle would be involved in this mission."

"Very good! You two sit tight, and I will get you going in the next forty-five minutes or so," Jonah explained, the anticipation of the mission palpable in his voice.

Eddie, his form weightless, hovered just behind Stella and Harold.

Barry and the girls sit in the water filtration room, their nerves palpable as they wait for news.

Jonah summons the Cigar-Man on his keypad in his control room in California.

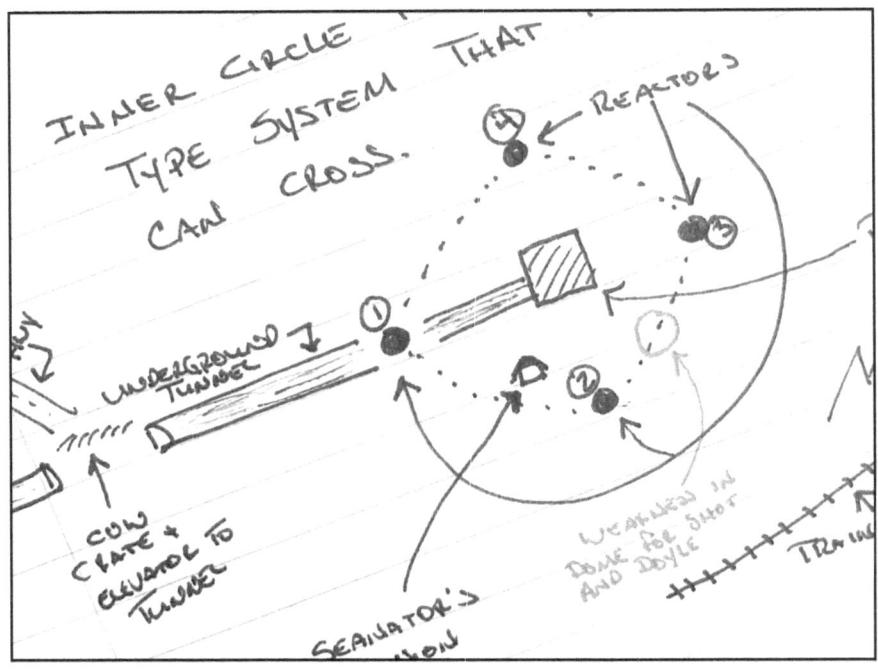

CHAPTER NINE

REVERSE ENGINEERING

"Up and Adam boys," Jonah's authoritative voice reverberates through the barracks that Doyle and Mike slept in last night, instilling a sense of seriousness.

Doyle rolls over and sees Mike, already dressed and ready to go, sitting on the edge of his bunk and looking at a small, handheld computer. "Did you sleep any?" Doyle asked.

"Like a baby. I'm ready to get this mission started so we can get it over with," Mike said, his impatience palpable.

"I just hope it goes as planned, and we get there before the Senator hurts Dad," Doyle said as he climbed out of his bunk, his determination shining through.

"From what I have heard about your dad, Barry, he can care for himself against the Senator. Listen to me, Doyle. You will go in alone once we arrive at the Senator's ranch. I have to stay back and watch

over the flying disk; from what I just read from Jonah, only one person can cross over the security system," explained Mike as Doyle started getting dressed.

Doyle's brow furrowed, "What kind of security system are we talking about here?"

Mike shook his head. "I have never seen anything like it. A dome-type field protects the inner circle of the ranch, where the Senator's house and the prison are."

"You mean like a force field?" asked Doyle.

"Yeah, you could say that. Jonah has made arrangements with one of the spies or bounty hunters we use to break the code on the security system at the ranch. According to the map Jonah included, there is one area that one person can cross that will not set off the alarm or, worse, won't electrocute you. Once you have rescued your dad, you can exit at any spot and be safe." Mike told him as he showed him the map on his handheld.

Doyle examined the map and looked up at Mike. "The Senator doesn't take any chances on his safety. Hell, the White House is not that secure."

"Brace yourself, Doyle. Who knows what horrors await you on that ranch? The Senator is a ruthless man!" Mike's words cut through the air with a sharpness that left no room for doubt.

"I'm bracing for the worst, Mike. And this, I believe, will be the last time we cross paths with the Senator." Doyle's voice held a note of finality as if he had already decided.

Mike swiftly turned towards the barracks' exit. "Remember, Doyle, the Senator is off-limits. We need to get moving; Jonah's waiting for us." His urgency was noticeable.

The two strolled down the familiar hallway; their curiosity piqued just as it was the first time Doyle saw this technological marvel. The place, as pristine as a hospital, bustled with the activity of military personnel and civilians, each contributing to the facility's enigma.

Mike stopped at an unmarked door, "This is our hangar, brother," he said as he punched on the keypad.

Doyle's anticipation was off the charts, his stomach churning with the unknown. The door slid open, and the two stepped into the Anteroom, their readiness to face whatever lay ahead evident.

Mike looked at Doyle, "We have to be clean before we can enter the hangar," he said with a smile.

As the room filled with fog and UV lights flashed, a buzzing sound filled the air. Unexpectedly, Doyle began to cough and sneeze, and then Mike did the same, their reactions mirroring each other.

The opposite door opens, and as both men step out, a mist of what smells like rubbing alcohol hits them in the face. They both rub their eyes as they move forward out of the fog.

"Well done, gentleman," Jonah says, standing in their path.

"What the hell was that all about?" Mike asked.

"It was more for you than anything. The chemical compounds we use on the disk could potentially make you ill. We have found that if we spray someone with that mixture that yours truly invented, you will not have any reactions to the disk," explained Jonah.

Doyle removed his hands from his eyes, and as his vision returned, he saw it. The flying disk, an otherworldly marvel, was sitting right before him. Its hull resembled alligator skin, with tiny windows adorning the top section. It sat on three legs that looked like they belonged to a dinosaur. A narrow ramp extended from the left side, reaching past the outer edge. Several cords were plugged into it in different locations, and steam slowly rose off the top, adding to its mystique.

"I have never seen anything like this in my life," Doyle said, his voice filled with awe at the sight of the flying disk, an otherworldly marvel, sitting right before him.

Doyle stood there gazing at the sight. "So, did you read over the paper I gave you?" Doyle turned to see the Cigar-Man, a pivotal figure in their plan, standing beside Jonah.

"What are you doing here?" asked Doyle.

Jonah walked up to Doyle and said, "This man has arranged a way for you to break the security code at the ranch."

"Doyle, the codes on the paper I gave you must be entered on the keypad on the third statue," the Cigar-Man explained, his voice carrying a hint of mystery. His enigmatic nature added to the intrigue of the task at hand.

"Statue?" Doyle asked.

The Cigar-Man nodded, "Yes. There are four of them arranged in a circle. They are reactors, each with its own keypad. Each is an eight-foot-tall granite statue of Greek gods strategically placed to form a security system. You must enter those codes on the third one and walk twelve paces toward the second statue. That position is where you can cross the invisible lasers that make up the dome."

Doyle tapped his chest pocket, "I've got it right here. The third one and twelve paces toward the second, 10-4." His voice was filled with a mysterious confidence that piqued Mike's curiosity.

"Perfect. It sounds like you will not have any problems. Good day, gentlemen," the Cigar-Man said, his voice a low, gravelly rumble that seemed to echo in the hangar. He turned and walked into the Ante-room, his long coat billowing behind him like a cape. He turned back and looked at Doyle as the fog made him vanish from sight.

"I've never trusted that guy," Mike snapped, his eyes narrowing with suspicion.

"Sometimes we have to use people that are not always good. But, if it's for the greater cause, I guess it's okay," Jonah replied, the weight of their crucial and perilous mission hanging heavy in the air.

The three guys stood staring into the Anteroom, a dimly lit chamber with walls adorned with spray nozzles, before Jonah spoke up again.

"We need to load you two onto the flying disk. I do have your things all packed into a backpack, Doyle," Jonah said as he walked over to a nearby table and picked up a camo backpack, a symbol of the mission's gravity.

Doyle reached out and grabbed the pack, "Thanks."

Jonah motioned for Mike and Doyle to follow him to the ramp into the disk. "I cannot go in and show you around, so I'll explain it from here. Once you reach the top of the ramp, you'll be in the outer ring of the disk. No one can be in this area, or the disk will not lift off. The pressure is so high that you will be killed in seconds if you are in this area. This outer ring is used only when the disk is on the ground."

"How do we enter the inner ring?" asked Doyle.

"In the front of the disk in the outer ring, there is a round door. You open that door and step through what looks like water or a mirror. It's hard to explain, but you'll understand once you get to that point. Do you have any questions?" Jonah asked.

"No more questions. Let's embark on this journey," Mike declared, his voice filled with anticipation as he led the way up the ramp.

Jonah placed a reassuring hand on Doyle's back. "You've got this, guys. Once you're in the cockpit, I'll be with you through the computer," he said, his voice brimming with confidence.

"Here we go," Doyle said, his voice tinged with excitement as he ascended the ramp.

Once at the top of the ramp, the two men entered the outer ring, which is only six feet high and roughly four feet wide. Both walked slightly slumped over to keep from bumping their heads. As they walked away from the ramp, it slowly started retracting and latched closed. The outer ring is lined with blue lights, slowly flashing red every six feet. Once the ramp latched closed, Doyle noticed a sudden change in pressure, causing his ears to pop, a sensation akin to ascending in an airplane.

Mike stopped when he reached the round door. The door was not level up and down, but it laid back on a forty-five-degree angle. "Are you ready for this, Doyle?"

"I was born ready, Mike."

Mike's hand trembled as he reached out and pressed the button beside the door. The door rolled to the right into the wall, and the watery, mirror-like substance gleamed in the blue lighting. Mike stuck his hand through. "It's warm," he told Doyle, his voice tinged with excitement.

"Go ahead, step through, Mike."

Mike looked back at Doyle, his hand still pushed through the watery substance. "Here goes nothing," he said as he stepped through. His figure quickly dissolves into the watery surface, disappearing from Doyle's view.

"Mike? Mike?" Doyle called to him, but he heard no response. Doyle's heart raced as he looked side to side and shrugged his shoulders. "What the hell?" he said, then practically leaped into the watery door, his mind filled with concern for what lay ahead on the other side.

Doyle tumbled to the ground on the other side of the door, his body a chaotic jumble of limbs. "Mind those steps; you'd reckon Jonah would've given us a heads-up about the drop," Mike chided, swiping a slime trail from his shoulder.

Doyle rolled over and looked at the steps, "It's three steps down, to be exact."

"You okay?" Mike asked.

"I'm good," Doyle said, showing his resilience as he stood up.

Mike pointed at his chin, "You have slime on your face."

Doyle rubbed his chin, "I wonder what this stuff is?"

The guys marveled at the interior of the inner ring, their eyes widening at the sight. They found themselves in a space that resembled a den, complete with an oversized horseshoe leather couch curved around the wall. Ladders led to a small upper section on either side of

the door they had just passed through. This upper section, they soon realized, was the cockpit, with four captain's chairs reclined and facing the ring of windows encircling the top of the flying disk.

"You guys, it's time to climb into the cockpit and choose a chair," Jonah's voice echoed over the intercom inside the disk, igniting a surge of excitement for the adventure ahead.

"After you," Mike told Doyle.

"Okay," Doyle replied, looking up at the ladder's top. He grabbed ahold of the ladder and climbed to the top. Once at the top, Doyle slid to his left and sat in one of the cockpit seats, feeling the comfort of the well-designed chair. Mike followed behind and sat in the chair next to Doyle.

Jonah's voice came over the intercom again: "Okay. Go ahead and strap the shoulder harnesses on. A pair of glasses is in the pocket on the side of the chair. You'll need to wear those if you plan on looking out the window, as we will be flying in the upper atmosphere."

"Jonah, what was that substance we stepped through in the doorway?" asked Doyle, his curiosity heightened by the mysterious substance.

"Doyle, that is classified, but I can tell you this: You both are now in a womb, for lack of a better word. That substance surrounds your entire pod, including between the double-layer glass in the cockpit. Because of that substance, you will feel very little motion while the

disk is in flight; if not, the g-forces implied to your bodies at moving over three thousand miles per hour would kill you almost instantly."

"Three thousand miles per hour?" Mike asked.

"You heard me correctly. It can also go 70 knots underwater, two times faster than a nuclear sub. Imagine the thrill of moving at three thousand miles per hour and 70 knots," replied Jonah, emphasizing the exhilarating speed.

Doyle looked at Mike and smiled, "Are we going under the water, Jonah?"

"Not unless we have to," replied Jonah.

"That's good to know," Mike said, strapping the harness over his shoulders, symbolizing their unity and trust in each other.

"Okay, gentlemen. Sit back and enjoy the flight to Wisconsin. Once we reach the Senator's ranch, the disk will hover directly over the landing spot at sixty thousand feet. Once I know the ground team is in position, the disk will land and let Doyle out. The disk will then return to sixty thousand feet, hovering until Doyle exits the ranch with Barry," Jonah explained, his determination apparent in his voice.

"How will we not be seen when the disk lands in Wisconsin?" Doyle asked.

"Excellent question. The disk will be in stealth mode, invisible to the human eye. However, you will not be invisible once you leave it,

Doyle. In most missions that use this disk, operators use one of our invisible suits to keep from being seen." Jonah explained.

"That's great. I'll look like a time jumper just appearing out of nowhere," Doyle replied.

The guys could hear Jonah laughing. "Doyle, you will be fine, I promise. I would not let you exit if anyone is near the landing spot. Now, gentlemen, on the left-hand side of your seats, there is a small cooler with food cubes and water. That is your breakfast, and you should eat it before you arrive in Wisconsin," Jonah told them.

The lights inside the disk dimmed, and the two guys could hear a slight humming as the disk slowly lifted off the hangar floor. The windows turned crystal clear, and the entire hangar came into view, a breathtaking sight. They could see a section of the wall in front start to open as the lights in the hangar went dark. In a sudden, unexpected move that caught them off guard, the disk darted out the open door and quickly gained altitude.

"Holy shit! That was fast," exclaimed Doyle as he looked out the windows down to the ground, which now looked forty thousand feet below. The sudden, exhilarating acceleration of the disk sent a thrill through him, making his heart race excitedly.

"How was that for power?" Jonah asked.

"That was awesome," Doyle said, looking over at Mike.

"Yeehaw," Mike replied with a hint of sarcasm.

"Sit back and relax; you'll be in Wisconsin in about thirty minutes. Oh, and eat your breakfast," Jonah told the guys.

"No turning back now, Mike," Doyle said as he opened the cooler and pulled out a bag of food cubes.

Mike turned and looked at him, shaking his head, "Looks yummy."

0730 HOURS ✳ CENTRAL DAYLIGHT TIME
PRESENT-DAY
RAILROAD TRACKS NEAR THE SENATOR'S RANCH, WISCONSIN

Stella and Harold felt the train come to a stop. They both looked outside and saw rolling hills, tall hardwood trees, and acres of pasture with cattle staggered about. Several red barns dot the landscape, and the homesteads are surrounded by white picket fencing.

"Wisconsin sure is beautiful, isn't it?" Stella asked Harold.

Harold nodded, his eyes gleaming with determination, "That it is. But we are not here to see the sights. We need to get our gear on and move out. It's time for this mission."

Jonah's voice came over the train's intercom, "You two ready?"

"We're all set," Stella confirmed, her voice tinged with determination.

"Jonah, I am ready to guard the train while they are gone," Eddie, the drone, said in his robotic voice.

Harold walked past Eddie and gave the drone a funny look, "I'll be glad to get away from this drone," he told Stella, who rolled her eyes

in response. "You know Eddie's just trying to help, Harold," she said, defending the drone.

"I am preparing to disrupt the power in that part of Wisconsin. This event will also turn off GPS and satellite signals. The power outage will last approximately ninety minutes, giving us a window to execute our mission. You have a mile from here to the bluff overlooking the Senator's house and entrance to the underground prison. As soon as the Senator is in sight, take the shot and evacuate," Jonah's voice crackled with urgency.

As soon as Jonah finished speaking, a sudden burst of thunder and lightning filled the sky, casting an eerie pink hue before returning to its standard color, leaving the team with a sense of unease.

Jonah's voice returned over the intercom: "That is your sign. The systems are down in Southern Wisconsin."

"Understood," Harold acknowledged, his voice steady and determined. The train door slid open, and he and Stella leaped out, ready to embark on their mission toward the Senator's ranch.

"Be safe, my friends," Eddie said as the train door closed.

0732 HOURS * CENTRAL DAYLIGHT TIME
PRESENT-DAY
UNDERGROUND PRISON AT THE SENATOR'S RANCH,
WISCONSIN

"I hear someone coming," Emily tells Barry.

"Everyone, please stay quiet and sit down," Barry's voice trembles as he tells the girls, who are now shaking with fear and hiding in the water treatment room.

They strain their ears, the sound of their breathing almost deafening in the silence. Heavy and purposeful footsteps echo down the hall toward the cell block. The crack of the loud light switches reverberates through the prison, and the sounds of the light ballasts pop as all the lights come to life, casting eerie shadows on the walls.

"Senator! We have a problem. All of the cells are empty," one of the FBI agents yells out.

"What the hell? Barry, you crusty old bastard!" the Senator yells.

"What do you want us to do, sir?" the second agent asks.

"Find them! They couldn't have gotten far, check all the rooms. They have to be in this cell block somewhere," the Senator's voice is urgent, almost desperate.

Thunder shook the complex before the agents could move, and the lights went dark. The backup systems also failed to restore the power to the underground prison. Undeterred, the Senator motioned for one of the agents to follow him back up top.

"You stay and continue the search for Barry and the girls. Our fate rests on your shoulders. We will try and restore power to this facility," the Senator commanded, his voice carrying the weight of their responsibility.

The Senator and his agent hurriedly left the prison, sprinting across the lawn towards his mansion. They swiftly entered a back entrance that led to the ranch's command center. The Senator quickly opened a large metal cabinet, "Good, the security dome is still operating. I invested over ten million dollars in this dome system and its battery backup system."

The agent, his handgun at the ready, turned to the Senator with a furrowed brow, "What about the rest of the systems and the electricity to the ranch?"

"They should have started automatically," the Senator replied, striding to the electrical panels and peering outside at the backup generators. "The generators should have started on their own. See if you can reach the electrician in town that we use."

The agent looked at his cell phone, "Sir. It appears I have no signal whatsoever."

"That's strange. Go try the satellite phone," the Senator said, shaking his head.

The agent left the room to find the satellite phone, his determination unwavering. The Senator walked outside to inspect the emergency generators when he noticed the odd color of the sky.

"If I didn't know better, I'd say that this is the work of the Patriot's Group," the Senator mumbled as he looked at the sky and surveyed the wooded bluffs surrounding the ranch. The Patriot's Group, an organization known for its disruptive tactics, had been a thorn in the

side of the Shadow Government for years. Their methods were ruthless, and their reach was far.

"Sir. The satellite phone is also useless," the agent yelled, his voice tinged with a hint of panic at the dire situation.

The Senator's voice was strained, "They are coming. We must restore the power if we can. We may have thirty minutes before the perpetrators arrive at the ranch. I have another small generator located in the storm cellar, which is lead-lined. If this was an EMP event, it should have been protected in that cellar." Despite the odds, the Senator was determined to fight back.

"Sir, I'll go get the generator. Where should I place it?" the agent asked.

"Bring it to the door to the electrical room. I have an outlet we can plug into to restore some lighting, but not all of it," the Senator explained.

"Senator, it's not safe for you to be out here. There could be someone nearby who might take a shot at you," the agent urged, his concern evident in his voice.

"I'm not afraid of that. You just go get that generator, agent," the Senator declared, his voice steady and unwavering.

"Yes, sir," the agent acknowledged his response, clearly displaying his respect for the Senator's authority.

```
0800 HOURS * CENTRAL DAYLIGHT TIME
PRESENT-DAY
BLUFF OVERLOOKING THE SENATOR'S RANCH, WISCONSIN
```

"Stay low, Stella. We can be seen now from the Senator's house," Harold warned her, the tension in his voice noticeable.

"Just relax. I like this spot right here, Harold," Stella replied, trying to keep Harold on point.

"I agree. You get set up, and I will look and see what is going on down there," Harold told her, pulling out his binoculars.

"Wait just a minute. How will we know when the dome system is disabled so I can take the shot?" Stella asked.

Right after she asked Harold that, a white owl landed beside them. It opened its wings to display a small screen on its chest with a message for them.

The message read: ***"Once you see Doyle enter the ranch directly below you. The protective dome will be disabled for twenty-five seconds. You must take the shot at this point. I will notify you when Doyle is disarming the system."***

"Good enough," Stella said as she laid her sniper rifle on the ground and got into her shooting position.

Stella lay there looking through the rifle's scope as Harold canvassed the area with his binoculars.

"Okay, Doyle. We are above the Senator's ranch," Jonah's voice said over his headset.

"That was very fast," Doyle replied.

"I told you it would be. Now, I'm going to set the flying disk down so you can exit and get to the Ranch's reactors and disarm them. The moment you turn off the protective dome and enter the inner circle of the ranch, you will hear the sniper shot. Your role is crucial, Doyle. You must act swiftly to rescue your dad. Understood?" asked Jonah, his voice carrying the weight of the mission.

"Understood," replied Doyle.

"The entire mission will only last fifteen minutes. Five minutes to get to the reactors, ten minutes to rescue your dad and any prisoners, and then five minutes to get them to the train. Remember, our objectives are clear: reach the reactors, rescue the prisoners, and board them onto the train for safety," explained Jonah, reinforcing the mission's goals.

Doyle nodded, "I've got it."

"Good. Now, brace yourself," Jonah said as the sleek, silver disk hurtled toward the ground. It plummeted from sixty-thousand feet to the ground in three seconds and landed as softly as a feather.

Eddie continued to guard the train.

The Senator and the agent worked on the backup generator.

Barry and the girls prepared for the other agent to find them.

CHAPTER TEN

THE BATTLE

---

08 15 HOURS ✻ CENTRAL DAYLIGHT TIME
PRESENT-DAY
THE SENATORS RANCH, WISCONSIN

"Open the door!" the agent demanded as he pounded on the door to the water treatment room.

Barry motioned for the girls to stay still. He slid over to Emily and said, "I'm going to open the door and let the agent in. When he steps in, I want you to hit him in the head with this pipe wrench."

Emily looked at the wrench and made a face as she took it from Barry, "Will that not kill him?"

"No. It will knock the agent out long enough for us to tie him up. We are also going to tape his mouth shut," Barry said, holding a roll of duct tape in his hand. Barry picked up the end of the cabinet blocking the door and moved it to the side, giving him enough room to open it.

"Okay…if you say so, Sir," Emily replied with the pipe wrench in hand. Barry used his hands to push Emily into the corner on the back side of the door as he slowly opened the door.

"What the hell is going on in there, and why are you out of your cell, old man?" the agent asked, stepping into the water treatment room with his gun in hand.

"I was thirsty and came here looking for water," Barry replied.

"What do you mean you were thirsty? You are not allowed out of your cell, old man," the agent said as he noticed all the girls sitting in the room. "What are you all up to?" he asked, turning to Barry.

WHAM!! Emily struck the agent in the side of the head. "What you up to….." the agent mumbled as he fell to the floor, dropping his pistol.

Barry reached down and grabbed the agent's pistol, "Damn girl! That was a home run."

"Help me tie him up and tape his mouth, girls," yelled Barry to the girls.

All the girls rushed to aid Barry and Emily by tying the agent up. Once they had him tied up, Barry stuffed a rag into his mouth and wrapped his head with duct tape.

"That should hold him," Barry told Emily, winking and smiling. "Girls, drag him to the back of the room, but do not hurt him further. We will let the law take care of him, and we will not act like

these guys do," explained Barry as he turned and walked through the open door and back into the cell block, which was pitch black from the power outage.

Barry reentered the water treatment room, "Emily. Hand me the flashlight that you found earlier."

Barry slowly entered the cell block, shining the flashlight around and checking to ensure no one was there.

DOYLE

Doyle stepped from the flying disk and jogged towards the ranch's reactors. Two robotic owls, crucial in scanning the area for soldiers in invisible suits, hovered twenty feet above him, their advanced computer software at work. The tension was high, and their vigilant eyes added to the intensity. Once the trio had cleared the thrust area of the flying disk, it ascended to sixty thousand feet above the ranch.

The ranch was a sight, with rolling hills and large trees starting to put out their leaves on this early spring morning. Doyle could see the Senator's mansion and what looked to be a significant red barn, which was the entrance to the underground prison. An eerie stillness in the air, so thick you could cut it with a knife, added to the intensity that Doyle felt pulsing through his veins.

Doyle approached reactor number two and then veered east towards reactor number three. He retrieved the note from his pocket, a cryptic message from the Cigar Man: "Once I enter the code, red lights will

start flashing. Once all the lights synchronize, enter the code." Doyle muttered the instructions, acutely aware of the two owls perched on reactor number three, their presence a chilling reminder of the secrecy shrouding his mission. As he waited, he saw the Senator and one of his agents working on something that sat on the ground. Doyle kept his body behind the reactor to keep the Senator from seeing him.

HAROLD & STELLA

"Stella, I have visual on Doyle at the reactor," Harold informed his sniper, his voice betraying a hint of concern for his friend below.

"Roger-that, Harold. I have the Senator in my sights," Stella replied, removing her eye from the rifle's scope and looking down at her son, Doyle.

"Do not fire until I see Doyle step over the security perimeter, and I will give you the okay," explained Harold.

"I understand, Harold," she replied, placing her head back onto the rifle and looking through the scope at the Senator.

DOYLE

"Okay, that is the sequence of lights I need," Doyle said, his voice tense as he entered the code on the panel of the third reactor. "Now, twelve paces toward the second reactor." Doyle watched the Senator and only started his steps when he was sure the Senator was not looking in that direction. The robotic owls left their perch as Doyle began

to take the required steps, his movements quick and precise. "Twelve. Here goes nothing," he said, his breath catching as he stepped across the perimeter between the two reactors. The owls remained outside the security perimeter, one perching on the number two reactor while the other owl returned to the number three reactor.

BOOM! The sudden rifle shot jolted Doyle, its echo reverberating through the rolling hills. He flinched, but his determination didn't waver as he continued toward the Senator's house. He saw the Senator drop, and the agent working on the generator jumped up and ran inside the home. Doyle's heart raced as he stopped running when he saw the Senator roll over and sit up. "Damn! The shot just grazed his head," Doyle said, his voice tinged with shock as he reached for his weapon.

When Doyle places his hand on his weapon, he is tackled to the ground. "What the hell," he said, rolling over to see a ghostly image of Colonel Miller standing over him.

"Do not move," Colonel Miller told Doyle.

HAROLD AND STELLA

"Target down," Stella reported to Harold.

"Great shot," Harold replied, still looking through the binoculars. He could see the Senator was not eliminated, and Doyle was lying on the ground looking up at nothing. "This is it, Stella. We must hurry to the train," he emphasized, walking over to help her pack her gear.

"I got him, correct?" she asked.

Harold continued to gather up their gear.

"Harold? Did I get him?" she asked again.

"Yes, Stella, you got him."

Stella smiled, "Good riddance, you old SOB. Payback for all the dirty deeds the Senator has done in his lifetime."

"Stella! Do not celebrate the Senator's demise unless you want someone to celebrate yours," Harold scolded her.

"You are right, Harold. My apologies"

Two whitetail robotic deer ran up to them, their sensors scanning the area for any sign of danger. Harold and Stella quickly exited the bluffs above the Senator's ranch, flanked by the vigilant deer.

DOYLE & COLONEL MILLER

"Yes, Doyle, it is me. Colonel Miller."

Doyle sat up, "How did you survive that hellfire on that mountain?"

"That I do not know. I didn't come here to chat with you. I am willing to put our differences aside for now so that you can rescue your dad. I will take care of the Senator and the two agents," Colonel Miller explained.

Doyle stood up and looked Colonel Miller in the eyes, "I'm sorry, buddy, that this happened to you."

"There's no time for apologies, Doyle. The clock is ticking. Now, go!" Colonel Miller urged as they heard the Senator's cries for help.

The Senator stood up, with blood running down the side of his head. "Doyle! You treacherous bastard! You shot me!" the Senator's accusation pierced the air when he saw Doyle standing nearby.

"Go! Now!" Miller yelled at Doyle. Then, in a sudden, swift movement, he leaped over and landed on the Senator's shoulders. Colonel Miller glanced at Doyle and then twisted the Senator's head around. Colonel Miller's eyes glowed red, and his voice sounded like a monster: "Go rescue your dad and the girls and exit the opposite way toward the train!" he said as the body of the Senator fell to the ground. Miller stood up, holding the Senator's head as he stared at Doyle.

The agent that ran into the Senator's home came out of the door, firing his weapon at Colonel Miller. The bullets didn't hit the Colonol but went completely through him and hit the side of the barn behind him as Doyle turned and ran into the prison door away from the gunfire. Colonel Miller turned and threw the Senator's head at the agent, knocking him to the ground, then started walking toward the agent.

Doyle closed the heavy prison door, the sound reverberating through the dimly lit cell block. He reached into his shirt pocket, his fingers brushing against the cool metal of a flashlight. As he flicked it on, the beam of light pierced the darkness, revealing his dad, Barry, and a group of girls clustered near the center of the cavernous room.

"Dad. Are you Okay?" Doyle asked.

"Yes, son, I'm good. It's nice to see you, especially in these circumstances," Barry said with a weary smile, his eyes betraying the fear he was trying to hide.

Doyle noticed more girls than he expected, "How many others do you have there?"

"Twenty-five girls total," Barry answered.

Doyle shook his head, "Damn, that is a lot."

The agent's scream outside pierced the tense atmosphere of the cell block. The girls all hurried away from the sound when Barry broke the silence, "What on earth was that?"

Doyle turned and looked toward the entrance door, "That would be Colonel Miller eliminating one of the agents."

"Colonel Miller? I thought he was dead," Barry started, his voice trembling with fear, before Doyle, the stoic leader of their group, cut him off.

"Yeah, well, me too. I'll explain later. We need to get out of here. We need to find the exit out that way," Doyle said, pointing towards a dimly lit corridor that seemed to stretch into the unknown.

Barry looked around, "Emily. Do you know how to get to that exit?"

Emily walked around a group of girls, "Yes. I know exactly where that is; follow me."

Doyle approached Emily and handed her the flashlight, "Lead the way, young lady."

Emily took the flashlight and smiled at Doyle, "I'd be happy to. We're in this together, right?" Doyle nodded, a flicker of trust passing between them.

"By the way, son. There is another agent tied and gagged in the water treatment room," Barry explained.

"Leave him there. Now, let's get moving," replied Doyle.

HAROLD & STELLA

"Excellent! You both made it back," Eddie, the drone, said as he saw Stella and Harold approaching the train.

"You didn't think we would?" Harold asked.

Eddie unlocked and opened the train door, "I knew you both would make it back."

Harold assisted Stella up the steps into the train and tossed their packs in. "Eddie, I have had just about enough of you. I don't want to hear another word from you until we get back to the train depot," demanded Harold.

"Yes, sir," Eddie replied.

"Harold! Will you please leave that drone alone? What is your problem with him anyhow?" Stella asked, her patience evident in her tone.

Harold looked at Stella and then at the drone, "I do not like robots," he said, his unease palpable.

Stella rolled her eyes, "You Indians are so superstitious," she said, her confidence in her modern beliefs clear.

"It is not normal for robots to talk to humans," Harold insisted.

"Eddie, I guess you should stay clear of him," Stella told the drone as she walked to the back of the train car and sat.

"Very well, Maam. I will prepare the train for the arrival of Barry Anderson and the girls," Eddie told her, then flew back outside.

DOYLE, HAROLD, AND THE GIRLS

"There is the exit," Emily said, pointing at the door. "That is the exit they move us girls into the tunnels. A ladder just past this door leads to a hatch near the train tracks."

Doyle walked to the door and turned the large latch, "It's locked."

"I have the keys," Barry declared, a glimmer of hope in his eyes as he held up a key ring with a dozen keys.

"Nice. How did you come to possess those?" Doyle asked.

"That's a long story, son," Barry replied, a hint of mystery in his voice.

"I bet it is. Well, just don't stand there, Dad; unlock the door," Doyle said, unable to hide his impatience but with a playful smirk.

Barry unlocked the latch, pulled the lever, and opened the large door. Cool air rushed through the opening, chilling the cell block tunnel. Doyle walked through the door and surveyed the extended tunnel, which was wet and slick at the bottom. He carefully walked to the ladder and looked up.

"Is there a lock on the hatch up above?" Doyle asked.

Emily shook her head, her uncertainty palpable. "I'm unsure about the lock on the hatch up above. It was open the night they brought me here."

"I see. The Senator uses the train tracks to bring in the kidnapped girls and drop them down this hatch. Sad," Doyle said, shaking his head in disappointment.

With a sense of urgency, Doyle climbed the ladder and pushed on the hatch, "Damnit, it's locked from the outside. We need to act fast, Dad." The situation was dire, and time was running out.

 Barry looked up the ladder at Doyle, "Are you sure, son?"

"Yes, Dad, I'm sure."

Barry turned to Emily, "How far does this tunnel go?"

"We can't go that way. This tunnel only leads to a dimly lit parking area where they load us into nondescript vehicles and then to an elevator that lifts the vehicles to the surface," explained Emily, her voice echoing in the confined space.

"Wait just a minute. I hear something outside that sounds like a grinder, "Doyle yelled down the ladder. He hears a snap and then a voice.

"Now push and the hatch," an unknown voice said.

Doyle pushed again on the hatch, and this time, it popped open. He slowly exited the tunnel hatch to see a tiny drone hovering nearby, which surprised him.

"Hello. Who are you?" Doyle asked.

"I am Eddie, the drone. My mission is to protect the train and to assist you in any way I can, Mr. Doyle. Jonah alerted me that you needed assistance with this hatch," the drone replied, relieving the team.

"Very good. Thank you, Eddie," Doyle said as he climbed out of the hatch and stood beside Eddie. He leaned over the open hatch, "Dad, start sending the girls up, but keep an eye out for any more agents." Their determination to rescue the girls was unwavering.

The first girl was halfway up the ladder when a blood-curdling scream pierced the tunnel's silence. The group froze, their hearts pounding in their chests, as they all turned to the source of the sound—the cell block. Barry, swift and decisive, rushed to the tunnel door and slammed it shut, the essential turning in the lock with a finality that echoed the urgency of their situation.

"This will only buy us a little time," Barry yelled to Doyle.

"That is all we need. It sounds like Colonel Miller found the second agent," Doyle told Eddie, who was still hovering beside him, the weight of the mission heavy in the air.

Doyle helped each girl out of the hatch with a steady hand and a reassuring smile. As Barry emerged, Doyle closed the hatch behind him, his actions seamlessly continuing their plan. Eddie, the drone at the ready, swiftly sealed the hatch with a welder that retracted from his underside and then turned to the group. "Follow me," he commanded, his voice a beacon of unity. "The train is just around the curve in the tracks."

When they saw the train, the group ran behind the drone down the tracks. The scene with the train looked like a Christmas card as snow started falling and quickly covered the ground. Harold stepped from the train to help the girls load up, their faces a mix of relief and anticipation.

"Harold, it's good to see you," Doyle said, walking to him and shaking his hand. Their camaraderie was evident in their firm grip.

"It's good to see you, too. You did a good job getting the girls out of prison," Harold replied.

"Thanks. Hey, who was the sniper working with you?" asked Doyle.

Harold looked into the train and then back at Doyle. "It was this drone," he said, pointing at Eddie, "that provided us with crucial aerial support during the mission."

"Really? He is not a good shot because he didn't take the Senator out," Doyle responded, looking at Eddie.

Hiding in a small room at the back of the train, Stella looked out the window at her husband and son. "This is a wonderful sight," she said to herself.

Barry, following at the end of the line, hugged Harold once the last girl loaded onto the train. "Thanks, brother, for coming to my rescue," he said, his voice choked with emotion.

Harold smiled, "Anytime, my friend."

"Dad, get onboard. I have to get this train moving and get out of here fast," Doyle explained urgently, pushing Barry up the steps.

Harold jumped on the steps as the train started moving, "Doyle, take care of yourself. I'll see you soon back in Tennessee!" he yelled as the train picked up speed.

Doyle turned to the drone Eddie, "You better get on that train too."

"Yes, I should. Jonah is very pleased with your work, Mr. Doyle," Eddie said. Then he darted to the train and entered the door, which closed as soon as he disappeared inside.

Doyle stood there, the urgency weighing heavily on him as he watched the train until it vanished into the snowstorm. The snow was falling in thick sheets, and the wind was howling. In the distance, a convoy of emergency vehicles was racing towards the ranch, their lights flashing in the blizzard. The distant sound of a helicopter added

to the chaos—the two robotic owls returned to his side, landing on the tracks nearby.

"Are you going to board, or are you going to just stand there?" Mike said, his voice tinged with urgency. He stood next to the enigmatic flying disk now visible due to the falling snow. Doyle could sense the worry in Mike's voice, spurring him into action.

Doyle turned and looked at Mike, "That thing is super quiet. I'm ready," Doyle said, jogging to the disk.

Doyle walked up the ramp into the flying disk, and Mike followed. The ramp closed as the two men entered, and then the disk returned to stealth mode, invisible to the human eye. The two robotic owls flew off in the direction the train was heading toward the Patriot's train depot.

As the flying disk lifted from the ground, a sudden snow tornado erupted from the thrust, a breathtaking sight amid the storm.

Colonel Miller stood on a nearby cliff, his eyes fixed on the enigmatic flying disk as it vanished into the snowy horizon, leaving behind a mystery trail.

Harold and Stella worked on feeding all the girls aboard the train.

INTERLUDE
DOYLE ANDERSON

The flying disk hovered in the vast upper atmosphere, a silent observer in the grand theater of space. The enormity of this space, with thousands of stars adorning the cosmic canvas, each one a unique masterpiece, is a sight that makes one feel small and insignificant in the universe's grand scheme. Below, thick masses of clouds obscured the earth, a stark contrast to the celestial beauty above. I can see both the Atlantic and the Pacific oceans from here.

As the disk reached its altitude, we paused, and Mike descended to the oversized couch, a mere mortal in the presence of such wonder. Is his inner ear thing bothering him again? I can't help but empathize with his struggle. He's been through so much in his lifetime, just like me. We share the constant juggle of work and family, the sacrifices we make, the moments we miss. I hardly see my two boys anymore, and the weight of that absence is a constant burden.

How did I get here? Just a year ago, I never would have believed a machine like this disk existed; its very existence is a puzzle that defies logic. If I hadn't answered that phone call to help in the search for the Wolfgang boy, I might be leading a completely different life. The mere thought of it is hard to understand. Perhaps my best friend would still be with us and not in protected custody.

And Colonel Miller, what in the hell is he now? A monster? The answer eludes me, shrouded in the fog of uncertainty, his transformation a mystery that keeps me on edge. But the way he attacked the Senator and took him out—I've never seen anything like that. The thought of him coming after Susan or me sends a chill down my spine. How will I stop him?

"Come in, Doyle. Do you have a copy?" Jonah's voice came over the intercom.

"Go ahead, Jonah, I hear you."

"How are you boys doing?" asked Jonah.

It seems Mike has succumbed to sleep, his body betraying his unwell state. "We're in the clear for now. Mike seems to be resting on the couch in a bad way. Jonah, I'm deeply concerned for him," I confessed.

"Mike, can you hear me?" Jonah asked.

"Yes. Can a man not get any sleep around here," Mike snapped, his irritation practically crackling in the air.

"Sure, you can sleep. All I ask is that you put a blood pressure monitor on your arm for the duration of the flight. The systems onboard will give you a good checkover, adjust the cabin pressure, and even inject any needed meds," explained Jonah.

"Right," Mike replied, his tone indicating his reluctance as he slid the blood pressure monitor up his arm. Then, he laid his head back down and fell fast asleep.

"Doyle, Mike will be just fine. I'm diverting us to one of our private islands in the South Pacific. It's the safest place for us right now," Jonah reassured.

"Really? Why is that?" I asked.

"The Shadow Government has put a price on your head for the killing of Senator Douglas. There is no place you will be safe other than this island," Jonah replied.

Like I needed more stress, "Okay, that sounds good, I guess."

"Rest assured, Susan is under the constant watch of our dedicated security detail. We've relocated her to a secure nuclear sub-terrain bunker four stories below the Edwards underground base. So, relax, and I'll meet you there in about forty-five minutes," Jonah reassured.

"Roger-that. Thank you. Doyle out," I replied, now fully aware of the urgency and gravity of my situation.

If the SG can't find me, will they go after my mom and dad or our boys? No, I'm sure Leon has that covered. His unwavering protection has always been a source of comfort for my family.

The stars now appeared blurred as the flying disk started moving again. The disk started glowing from the heat it generated in the upper atmosphere. I close my eyes to rest as we travel to the island, but I can't shake the anticipation of the battle ahead.

Doyle lays his head back and drifts off to sleep.

CHAPTER ELEVEN

WHERE ARE WE

Doyle and Barry drive to Louis Lee's trailer, which is parked in a small trailer park around a large lake in the mountains, and park in his driveway.

"I've always thought this lake was nice," Barry says, looking across the lake that has fog patches hanging over it.

"Yeah, it's a good area," Doyle replies, walking up the path to Louis' trailer.

"What in the hell is this?" Barry asks, pointing at the significant dent on the side of the trailer just before the steps leading to a small deck.

Doyle studies the dent, then looks around on the ground, "Don't move an inch, Dad." Doyle squats down and looks at several shotgun shells lying on the ground.

"Look at these shells scattered all about; it was like he was shooting in all directions," Doyle says, looking over at Barry. "Holy shit, Dad, he was shooting in all directions."

"What is it? I don't know what that means, son?"

"He was shooting at something he couldn't see. That is what it means, Dad. He was shooting at something cloaked."

Barry removes his hat and rubs his head, "That damn devil came after Louis!"

"I'd say so," Doyle says as he looks for clues about what happened here. Doyle walks around the area, up the deck's steps, and then looks at Barry.

"He shot from inside the house first because the glass was blown out onto the deck. Then, something or someone was thrown against the side of the trailer. Then he started shooting in all directions, and it looks like he headed this way," Doyle says as he returns down the steps and walks towards the tree line.

As he approaches the first tree, he sees a familiar mark on the ground: a distinct pattern that he had seen near some of Allen's tracks. "Dad, I saw this indention near some of Allen's tracks in the Smoky Mountains while searching for him. We need to find Louis as soon as we can; I fear Colonel Miller will kill him too!"

"That devil sum-bitch," Barry says, tapping the top of his .45 revolver under his jacket. "I'm ready to catch this thing and give it a little payback!"

"Colonel Miller sent his guys here because Louis saw something they don't want him to talk about," Doyle says as he pulls his phone out of his pocket. He dials Louis' number while Barry heads back down the path to the truck.

"I'm going to see if Willy heard anything last night," Barry shouted to Doyle before turning to Louis' neighbor's trailer.

"Where are you, Louis?" Doyle asked.

"Hey, Doyle. I'm almost to the overlook on Pinnacle Peak. Mandi called and said she came here to relax, but her car will not start now. Which is odd because she was heading to the store in Silva, North Carolina," Louis explained.

"That is the opposite direction by twenty miles or more. Louis, it sounds like a setup; we're on our way. You stay there and wait for us," Doyle told Louis.

"I'm at the pinnacle now. I will wait for you, Doyle."

"I'll be there in fifteen minutes," Doyle said; he placed his phone back into his pocket and jogged down the path to his truck.

Doyle and Barry hastily jump into the truck, and Doyle accelerates out of the driveway. "Louis just got a text from Mandi. She's stranded at the overlook on Pinnacle Peak, and her car won't start. Pinnacle Peak is in the opposite direction from which she is heading. Louis also said he went to the sheriff's office last night to report what attacked them last night," Doyle explains to Barry, the urgency in his voice palpable.

"Yeah, that's what Willy told me while you were talking to Louis on the phone," says Barry.

"Louis said he spoke to Officer Wong," Doyle says as he looks at Barry. "I've never heard of him, Dad. Have you?"

Barry shakes his head, "I have not."

"I think he is one of Miller's men, and now they know Louis saw the devil thing. I know now without a doubt that it's a suit of some type," replies Doyle.

"They're going to whack him now, son...step on it," Barry says urgently, pulling his .45 out to check that it's fully loaded.

Doyle looks at him, "Dad, you let me take care of this. I want you to stay in the truck because it may get ugly."

"Okay, I'll cover you, son. I like ugly."

Doyle turns his emergency flashers on and puts the pedal down, "Call the sheriff and get them out there. We might need as much firepower as we can get."

"I'm on it," Barry replies, pulling out his phone.

The short fifteen-minute drive feels like hours. Doyle stops the truck as they pull off the paved road onto the gravel road to the overlook.

"Dad, climb into the back seat. If there are shots fired, you lay down on the floorboard. Understand?" Doyle asks.

"Okay," Barry replies, climbing into the back seat.

Doyle opens the door, steps out, and walks to the toolbox in the truck bed. He swiftly pulls out an armored vest and puts it on, his movements precise and determined. He checks the pockets to ensure the extra clips for his 9mm are there, then gets back in the truck. "Here we go," he says, his voice steady and unwavering.

Doyle takes off slinging gravel as they round the final curve before the overlook; he sees Louis' truck with both doors open. He sees two men fighting with Louis in the front seat. He slams the brakes, "Back away from him now!" Doyle yells as he pulls his 9mm out and fires two shots into the ground just short of the truck.

"Get down, Dad," Doyle yells as he runs to the nearest tree.

The two guys jump out of Louis' truck and start firing rounds towards Doyle and his vehicle. Doyle returns fire from behind the tree, hitting one of the men in the leg. A black SUV comes racing around the curve from the opposite side with Colonel Miller behind the wheel. Doyle fires two shots at the SUV before he realizes that it has bullet-proof windows. He then tries to shoot out the tires, but they are puncture-proof.

Barry jumps out of the truck and runs to its rear. "Damnit, Dad, I told you to stay put!" yells Doyle.

"Don't bitch at me, just shoot those sum-bitches!" Barry yells to Doyle.

Barry leans out and unloads his .45 towards the SUV. The two men are behind Louis' truck now, with one of them wounded. Colonel Miller pulls over, blocking Doyle and Barry's view of his two hitmen.

"Keep shooting, Dad. We need to try to give Louis cover."

Doyle and Barry constantly fire at the SUV while Miller tries to load his men in the back seat. After they climb in, Miller slams the pedal down and starts to pull away.

Doyle sees the back window roll down just a few inches, "Get down, Dad!"

Machine gun fire rips up the ground in front of the tree Doyle is hiding behind, then it turns towards his truck and blows out his front tires. After the SUV goes out of sight, Doyle runs to Louis' truck. "Louis!" he yells out.

He investigates the truck and sees Louis lying on the front seat with his right arm pointed at his right temple. He climbs into the car and checks his pulse. Barry walks up to the passenger's side, "Is he alive?"

"Yes," replies Doyle.

Two police cars race around the curve with their sirens and lights on. Barry motions for them to pull up near Louis' truck. "Damn, it took you guys long enough!" he yells to them.

"We came right after we got off the phone with you, Barry," the sheriff (Bob) explains.

Doyle sits Louis up, "Can you hear me?"

Louis slowly opens his eyes, "They injected something up my rear... man."

"Dad, tell them to get an ambulance here ASAP. I think they tried to overdose him!" Doyle yells as he inspects Louis' arm because it's staying bent. He rolls up the sleeve of Louis' flannel shirt to see some device strapped to his arm.

"Doyle, an ambulance is on the way. What the shit is that thing?" Barry asks after seeing the bracket strapped to Louis' arm.

Doyle removes the bracket, "This dad is a suicide bracket. They install it under the shirt or jacket to keep from messing up the blood splatter. They place a pistol in the victim's hand and somehow stimulate the nerves, causing them to pull the trigger. I'm unsure how they remove it without disturbing the blood splatter.."

"Sweet Jesus, what is this world coming to?" Barry asks.

"Dad, grab on to him and help him remain sitting; I need to talk to the sheriff," Doyle told him.

Doyle walks over and hands the device to the sheriff, "Bob, they were in a black SUV with bullet-proof windows. They opened fire on us, and we returned fire, hitting one of the guys in the leg."

The deputy who arrived with the sheriff, his eyes steely and determined, swiftly got in his car and headed off after the black SUV. Doyle, meanwhile, walked to his truck and retrieved an old cigar tube and some tissue. He then walked to the front of Louis' truck, looking for any blood on the ground.

"Here we go; wow, he's bleeding good," Doyle says to himself as he leans down and pats blood onto the tissue, then tries to scoop up a little. He puts the tissue in the tube and puts the plastic top back on it. He hands the tube to Barry, saying, "Here, you know what to do with this. Also, call Harold to see if he can look at this site."

"Okay, son," Barry replies.

Doyle gets back in the truck beside Louis, "Hey buddy. Did you hear from Mandi before these guys attacked you?"

"No," Louis whispers, his voice barely audible, his face pale and drawn with pain.

"Dad, please tell the sheriff we need to find Mandi as soon as possible," Doyle pleads.

"Of course, son," Barry assures, walking to the sheriff.

"Hang in there, buddy," Doyle reassures Louis as he sees the ambulance pulling up behind them, his voice filled with concern and compassion.

Doyle helps the paramedics load Louis into the ambulance, "He told me they injected something into his rear-end. Probably trying to make it look like an overdose."

"Okay, we'll take good care of him," the medic replies.

The sheriff walks up to Doyle and says, "I'm going to need you to come down to the office in the morning to file a report on this. Also,

I have two wreckers on the way—one for your truck and the other for Louis'."

"Thanks. I'll be down there in the morning. Have you put out an all-points bulletin for Mandi and her car?"

"Yes. My office is working on it now."

"Louis had told me that she was going to the grocery just outside Sylva on Highway 107," Doyle explains.

"We'll find her; I'll have my guys search the entire route," the sheriff declares with determination, instilling a sense of resolve in Doyle.

0940 HOURS
PRESENT-DAY
UPPER ATMOSPHERE OVER NORTH AMERICA

Doyle sits up in the chair, his eyes drawn to the window of the enigmatic flying disk. It's a vessel that defies all known laws of physics, hovering between the stars and clouds below. He rubs the top of his head, still reeling from the jolt that woke him, only to find Mike standing behind him.

"You having another one of your medical episodes?" Mike asks, his voice tinged with genuine concern for Doyle's well-being.

"Why do you ask?"

"Because you were talking in your sleep, going on about finding Mandi. Who is Mandi?" Mike's curiosity is palpable in his voice.

Doyle straightens up in the cockpit chair, "She was my best friend's girlfriend."

Mike looks confused, "Was?"

Doyle looked at Mike, "Colonel Miller had her executed."

"I'm sorry about your friend's girlfriend. Colonel Miller seems to have left a long trail of dead people behind him." Mike replied as he looked out the window of the flying disk. "Looks like we are almost there."

"There is a lot of ice below us," Doyle said, looking out the window.

"We are crossing over, and then we will drop in altitude. That is Antarctica you are looking at, Doyle."

"Antarctica? Are we going to our base there?" asked Doyle.

Mike smiled, "No. We are going beyond Antarctica into the tropics."

"There are no tropics beyond Antarctica, Mike."

"Buckle up and sit back. Just watch and enjoy the show. What you will witness is a rare sight, a privilege granted to very few." Mike explained, underlining the rare privilege of their journey. Mike typed on the control panel's keypad, turning on the monitors with a view from the bottom of the disk so they could see the ground below.

The two men were on the edge of their seats as the flying disk they were riding in slowed and turned up at a 45-degree angle. Buffeted by extreme turbulence, the disk started bouncing and jerking side to

side. It glowed a bright red and then leveled out, revealing a breathtakingly beautiful blue sky outside. They started a slow descent, their anticipation mounting with each passing moment.

"I have never seen a sky so blue and an ocean so green; it's an amazing view," Doyle told Mike.

"There is no place like it on earth, Doyle."

"Have you been here, Mike?"

"I have, but only once. The flying disk is the new and improved way to get here. Before this disk was commissioned, the only other two ways to come here were from space on one of the Apollo or Space shuttle missions or by submarine. The submarine path to this island is not for the faint-hearted, and the submarine and her crew are subjected to extreme pressures. That is how I damaged my inner ears by coming here on a sub," Mike explained, underlining the challenging nature of the journey.

As they descended, they saw a giant storm off to the east, ascending from the ocean to the upper atmosphere, with lightning flashing. Large waves rolled around the storm, which appeared to be a thousand feet tall.

"There is a storm moving in," Doyle said to Mike.

"No. That storm is stationary. There is an island there, and the storm protects it and keeps anyone from accessing it," explained Mike.

"My goodness. Those waves are crazy tall. What could be on that island?" Doyle's curiosity piqued, and he turned to Mike for answers.

Mike turned to Doyle, "Jonah will explain that to you."

The flying disk descends through a large, fluffy white cloud, and the island below comes into view. They are greeted by rolling hills of bright green grass and towering buildings that seem to touch the sky. Flying vehicles zip around the structures, and several other flying disks glide alongside them. Doyle's eyes widen as he spots a launch pad with two sleek, futuristic Space Shuttles poised for lift-off.

"I thought they retired the Space Shuttle?" Doyle asked Mike.

"Another one of the lies our government told it's sheep. Those are not the older Space Shuttles, but our new models," Mike replied.

The flying disk approaches the landing pad as the two escort disks dart opposite directions. Doyle sees Jonah standing on a platform near the landing pad with four tall men beside him.

"Those guys look over seven feet tall," Doyle said, turning to Mike, his curiosity piqued by their unusual height.

"They are nine feet tall, actually," Mike replied, switching off the monitors on the control panel, his words leaving Doyle in a state of disbelief.

"Who are they?" Doyle asks.

Mike turned to Doyle, "They are the ones we work for," his tone indicating the significance of these towering figures.

The flying disk lowers its landing gear and touches down on the landing pad, which hangs out over the ocean two hundred feet below. Mike and Doyle climb down from the cockpit and gather their gear. They step through the doorway substance once again and walk around the outer corridor to the ramp, which is just now lowering.

"The next step in your training is about to unfold," Mike announced to Doyle, igniting a palpable spark of anticipation in the air.

"I'm absolutely thrilled," Doyle responded, his enthusiasm practically crackling in the air.

Jonah and his host descend a grand marble staircase, its steps adorned with intricate carvings, to the landing pad, where they wait to greet Mike and Doyle warmly.

CHAPTER TWELVE

WELCOME TO ATLANTIS

"Mike and Doyle, welcome to Atlantis," Jonah said as the duo stepped from the flying disk.

"Good to see you again, Jonah," Mike replied.

Doyle is spellbound by the view of the buildings surrounding the landing pad. From the ground, the buildings appear lined with gold siding that glitters in the sunlight. The air seems much more precise than anywhere he has been, and his sinuses also seem more transparent.

"Doyle, welcome, my friend," Jonah repeats.

Doyle turned to Jonah, "Yeah, thanks. Where in the world are we?"

Jonah smiled, "You are in Atlantis. The lost city of old."

"Right…Atlantis was destroyed and sank according to legend," Doyle replied.

"Correct. How better to hide it than to mislead generations from looking for it? The event that supposedly sank her only made the island safer from the outside world. And, Doyle, as you can see, the island is protected by an ice wall and turbulence that no known aircraft can navigate," explained Jonah, his voice tinged with secrecy.

Doyle turned to look at the distant ice wall, "How high does that ice reach?"

"It stands at an incredible height of twelve thousand feet. The wall you see is the outermost ice wall. There are shorter ones closer to Antarctica that keep most humans away. In the 1940s, the United States Navy found an underwater tunnel that leads to this island. However, it wasn't until the 1990s that man could navigate it successfully," explained Jonah, emphasizing the island's isolation.

"Unbelievable," Doyle said, shaking his head.

"But don't worry about all of that now; you'll have plenty of time to learn all about it in the classes I have set up for you in the coming days on the island," Jonah told Doyle, reaching out and putting his arm around him.

"If you say so, Jonah."

"I want you to meet our four top officers behind General X within the Patriot's Group," Jonah said, pointing at the nine-foot-tall gentlemen. "I'll start with the highest ranked to the lowest. Our leader who only answers to General X is Marshal Lesus—followed by Lieutenant

General Naza. We have Vice Admiral Rex, and lastly, to finish off the Patriot's Group command, is Commodore Luda."

The four officers walked over one by one and shook Doyle's hand. "Nice to meet all of you," Doyle told them.

The four officers remained silent, their inscrutable expressions adding to the mystery. They nodded, turned, and walked away. Mike walks over to Doyle and pats him on the shoulder. "Don't feel bad; I've never heard them speak either."

"They rarely speak. General X will take care of the speaking. Those guys do not speak English; they do not speak any of the world's languages. Their language is a dangerous force, capable of damaging your hearing without the proper protection," explained Jonah, his tone serious.

Doyle laughed, "Things just keep getting weirder by the minute. I do, however, have a few questions. One is why I am here on this island, and the other is what that large storm to the southeast of us is." Doyle asked.

"Doyle, your safety is at stake here. The Shadow Government has a target on your back for the death of Senator Douglas. We're doing everything we can to convince them of your innocence. And we're also working to clear your father's name of the false accusations the Senator was trying to pin on him," Jonah said, his voice tinged with urgency as he walked over to the edge of the landing platform and leaned on the railing.

Jonah raised his hand and motioned for another of his assistants to come down the stairs to the platform. "As for your second question. That storm surrounds the island where Dr. Furcus lives."

Doyle joined Jonah at the railing, looking down at the ocean waves crashing on the poles holding the platform up. "Who is Dr. Furcus?" he asked.

"Dr. Furcus is one of the Watchers, or Fallen Angels, that were locked in chains on that island," responded Jonah, reaching out and grabbing a newspaper from his assistant.

"The book of Enoch Watchers?" Asked Doyle.

"That is correct, Doyle. We have been working on gaining access to that island for decades. The only known way is a tunnel from Antarctica, guarded twenty-four-seven by the Watchers. That island is believed to hold many of the world's missing people, the ones that vanished without any traces," Jonah explained, handing Doyle the newspaper.

Doyle unfolds the newspaper and reads the front page number one story:

Senator Douglas found dead on his Wisconsin ranch.

Local authorities found the ranking Senator from Tennessee early yesterday morning, responding to a 9-11 call from the ranch. According to an anonymous source at the ranch, two federal agents were also found deceased at the ranch. A large number of prison

cells were also located underground in what looks to be connected to a worldwide sex trafficking operation.

"Oh my. We've finally exposed what the Senator was up to," Doyle replied after reading the headline.

"That is tomorrow's newspaper headline that will run worldwide. But don't be too sure of it convincing people. The Shadow Government will spin it in their favor, which is what we are working on. If we can clear you from that, then you can continue to work on search and rescue missions out in the open," Jonah explained.

"What if you cannot clear my name?" Doyle's voice trembled with uncertainty.

Jonah handed him a second newspaper, which his assistant had handed him. Doyle gave the first paper to the assistant and grabbed the second paper. He opened it and read the front page:

Highly decorated Army veteran Doyle Anderson killed in the Crazy Mountains.

Doyle Anderson was killed in an apparent fall in the Crazy Mountains, Montana. Anderson was in the region searching for a lost couple when he slipped and fell one hundred and fifty feet to his death. In a cruel twist of faith, upon hearing of her husband's death, Susan Anderson passed away due to her body being weak from complications of Mesothelioma. She was diagnosed with the disease in 2013 from working at ground zero as

an EMT in the aftermath of the terrorist attack on September 11, 2001.

"This can't be real," Doyle muttered, his hands trembling as he read the newspaper.

Jonah took the paper from Doyle, his expression unreadable. "This is the reality we're dealing with. We keep moving as is if we can convince the Shadow Government that you played no role in the Senator Douglas attack. If we can't...you remain here on Atlantis," he explained calmly.

"You can't be serious. You expect me to accept this and live my days on this island?" Doyle's voice was filled with disbelief.

"No, not at all. You continue doing what you're doing, but to the world, you are dead. You can only contact the people we allow. We will move Susan here, where she can get the medical attention she needs. Plus, the lack of pollution here will allow her to live a long and happy life. Both of you will live out your life here with us when you are not on a search, that is. There are also many celebrities that have faked their deaths to come live here." Jonah told him.

"What about our boys? They live without a mother and father?" Doyle asked.

Jonah turned and faced the ocean. "They are both grown men. We give them the option to remain in the known world or move here to this super-advanced world. But let's relax for the next few hours and

see how the Shadow Government reacts to Senator Douglas's death. Then we shall decide our path forward."

Mike walks over to the two guys and says, "Jonah, let's show Doyle around the island while we wait for any news from the SG. Also, you need to tell him about Louis Lee."

"What about Louis?" Doyle asked.

Jonah smiles, "That's right, I almost forgot. We are having lunch with your best friend, Louis Lee. He is here, Doyle. This island is where we put him into protective custody. He signed the paperwork to remain here for the remainder of his time."

"That's great!" exclaimed Doyle.

"You are right, Mike. We have about an hour to show Doyle the island's highlights before Susan arrives for lunch," Jonah replied.

"How are you getting Susan here?" asked Doyle.

"We put her into a deep sleep, and she's aboard another flying disk and will be on her way soon. Now follow me; I want to show you how we power this island with free energy," Jonah said, motioning for Doyle to follow.

The three men ascend the marble staircase to street level, away from the landing pads. Jonah walks in between Mike and Doyle, wrapping his arm around both as the entire city unfolds. The sight is not just breathtaking; it's awe-inspiring. Flying vehicles zoom overhead, their air-brake lights reflecting off the gold-painted sidewalk,

and the city's grandeur stretches out in all directions, a testament to other world ingenuity and progress.

THE END, FOR NOW.

www.ingramcontent.com/pod-product-compliance
Lightning Source LLC
Chambersburg PA
CBHW031258170626
46807CB00001B/202